NATASH

Send Me Home For Christmas

24-11-22

To Michael + Theresa

Wishing you love, laughter
+ Christmas miracles
xx
love

Natasha Kasis

First published by Diamond Roads 2022

First edition

ISBN: 978-1-8380652-5-6

This book was professionally typeset on Reedsy.
Find out more at reedsy.com

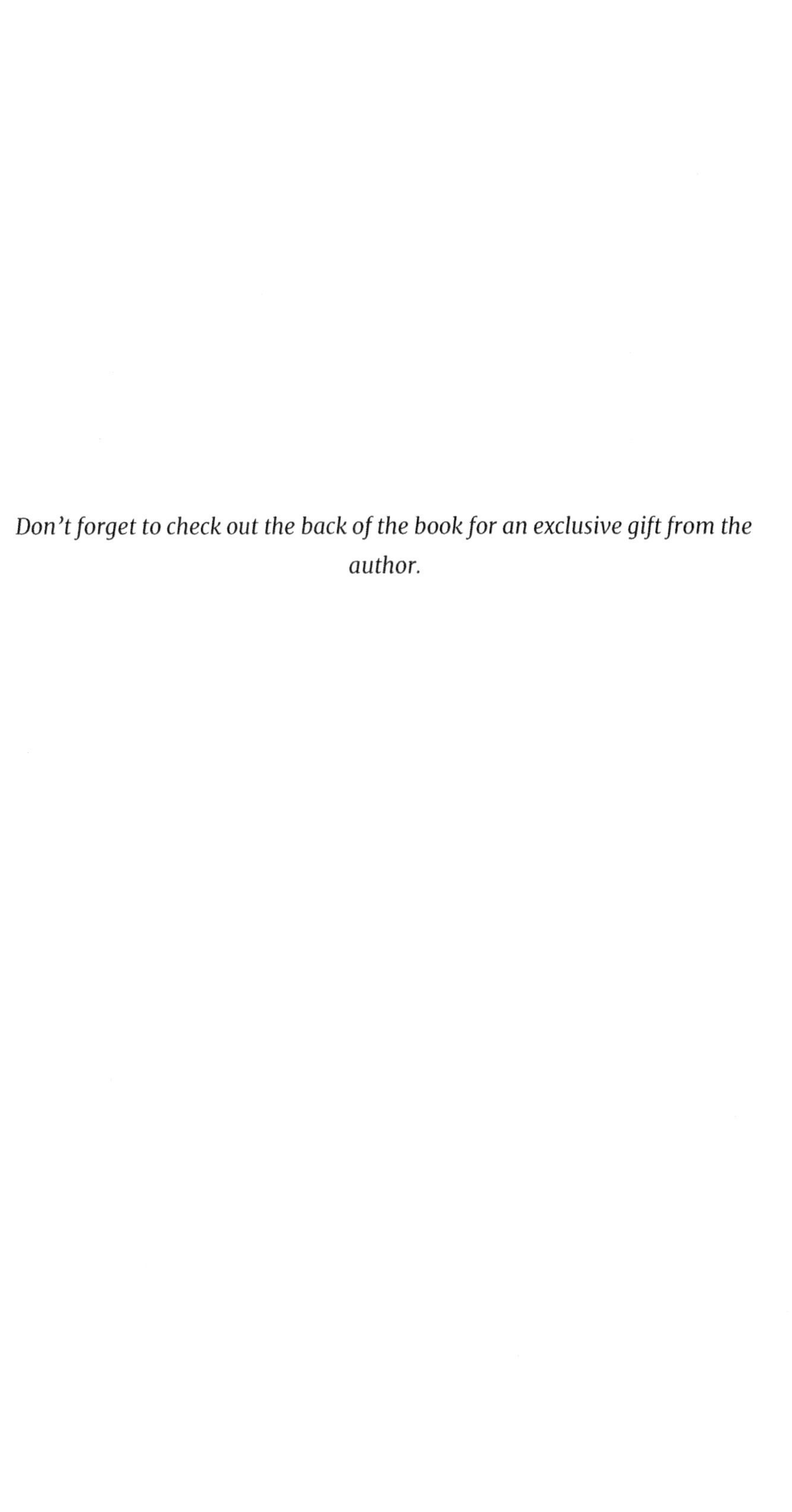

Don't forget to check out the back of the book for an exclusive gift from the author.

Contents

The sneak

I dressed in the dark. Careful not to make a sound, I knelt on the unfamiliar floor and felt around for the rest of my discarded clothes, wincing when I dropped a shoe. The worst thing I could do was wake him. I couldn't handle the awkward goodbyes, or the begging, or the way he looked at me as I left. It was better to slip out, to avoid the conversation. There was no more need for words.

Even though it was too early, when I was out of earshot of the room and way down the hotel corridor, I took out my phone and rang home. The landline rang and rang and the message service clicked on. The guilt urged me to speak; I needed to explain, and it was better to talk to a machine than say it in person.

'It was a mistake. I shouldn't have left, I'm sorry. I'm coming home.'

Even though it was morning and empty of any sign of life, the reception area had an impressive fire going and a Christmas tree bigger than my entire living room, full of intricate and expensive looking gold and silver decorations right in the middle of the hotel's foyer. As I approached the reception desk, a girl appeared from behind a door as if expecting me. The young receptionist was about twenty, and dressed in a black suit that labelled her Ruby. Scraped back from her face, her high ponytail gave her eyes a catlike, stretched appearance, this, coupled with full on makeup, made her look much older. She took my keycard from me and began checking me out.

'How was your stay Mrs. Goodman?' Ruby's English accent was typical of the London area, although she put on a posh lilt, probably expected more than gained.

I hesitated at the Mrs. It felt like a shot in the heart after leaving that room. Ruby noticed and her eyes grew wide in alarm. My first reaction was to put her at ease, I didn't have any want to make her feel bad.

'It was lovely, thank you.'

Ruby relaxed and went about her normal business of finishing checking me out.

'Are you working for Christmas?' I asked, more for small talk and to keep the girl moving than anything else.

She smiled and forgot the posh lilt. 'Yeah. I don't mind though. We have a rota and take turns for who's on. It was my year off but Carmel's little one is sick so I swapped. It don't bother me, I don't have kiddies. A mum should be with her family on Christmas Day.' Her face slackened when she saw my stricken face. 'Sorry, I...'

I gathered myself. 'Don't be. At all. That's very kind of you to do that for a friend.'

Ruby blushed, then shrugged. 'Isn't that what Christmas is all about?'

'Yes,' I said, feeling my own cheeks burn.

Ruby leant nearer. 'Besides, they put on a great day here. There's a party for all the staff and their family on Christmas morning, so even though I'm working, I get to see my parents and little brother and sister all dressed up, and they make such a fuss of them. Then, after we serve all the guests, we close for ages and have a feast. They put us up in the best rooms in the hotel, I get double time and three days off in a row and New Year's. I look forward to that more than anything. Christmas when you're single isn't so great, it's kind of lonely, actually.' She trailed off for a moment. 'It's more fun to watch the families staying here. I'll make it up to my family on Boxing Day and celebrate then.'

'Your friend is lucky to have you.'

The girl shrugged. 'She's had a tough year. She could do with something going right for a change.'

'Couldn't we all? Well, I hope you have a lovely Christmas and an even better New Year.'

Ruby's eyes flickered to my empty hands. I hadn't even packed a suitcase in my rush to leave, only catching the flight with a large handbag that contained little else than a change of clothes and some makeup.

'Where will you spend Christmas? In Ireland?' She asked.

I nodded. 'Home. I'm going home,' I said. 'Could you ring me a taxi?'

'Sure,' Ruby said, picking up the phone.

'Have you got a bathroom here I could fix myself up in before I go?'

Ruby puckered her lips and nodded her head, giving me a look that said she knew exactly why I needed to fix myself up somewhere other than my hotel room. It was a smile without judgment and for that, I liked her even more.

'Just down the hall and around the corner. It's the first door on the right. We won't clean the room straight away either,' she said, winking at me.

As I waited for my taxi outside the hotel entrance, I tightened my coat and wrapped a scarf around my neck. My breath made sharp lines that cut through the winter air. The heatless sun peaked out from above the horizon through the trees in the hotel's car park. The snow sparkled like diamond icing dusted on the surface. I resisted the urge to check my watch; there was plenty of time before I needed to be at the airport. The taxi arrived within minutes.

The snow had first fallen yesterday, two days before Christmas Eve. At first, I hadn't taken it seriously; it had been little flakes of fluff that melted before they touched the ground, not staying, just waiting to dry out. As I noticed them while looking out the hotel room's window, my thoughts occupied on whether there would be a knock on the door. Back then, the flakes took on a magical stance, full of promise, full of hope. I took more notice in the middle of the night, when I stood on the balcony, trying to catch my breath from the heat in the room, needing a moment to gather my thoughts from what had just happened, from what I had just done. By then the snow had thickened and was falling faster, growing strength on the concrete floor until it condensed enough to leave footprints. That was the first time I'd worried about my decision; the snow spreading an icy fear in my heart that I may regret coming. But still the warmth of the room called me, or rather, the warmth of the body lying waiting for me did.

In the morning light, I cursed the snow-capped trees and icy patches, and the continuing snowfall. The guilt mingled with my view and tainted it and I saw the snow for what it was; an obstruction and a nuisance between where I was and where I needed to be.

As the taxi drove me to the airport, we passed kids that weren't mine making snowmen, or footprints or snow angels, their bodies imprinting the ground and leaving black against the white, conjuring a feeling low in the pit of my stomach, a tugging pull towards home.

I smiled on seeing a man with a head-to-toe snow suited child on a snow sled, his hands hovering but not touching the boy, trying to keep up as the sled moved through the snow. The tight panic on the man's face was the reason for my smile, knowing he was a kindred spirit, knowing if it was me there standing over Ellie, I would try not to make a fuss either; to let her just enjoy the moment, but inside worrying about hypothermia or frostbite or slips. They don't tell you that about motherhood - from the moment your baby is born, you will never fully relax. You will never have another moment in their company when you can completely shut off, when there won't be some threat or hidden danger. Whether conscious or subconscious, from the day they land in your arms, you will be on alert for sounds or lack of sounds, for warning signals or alarm bells.

Couples passed arm in arm with woolly hats and snow boots. A bunch of teenagers stood at the top of a hill, tying a bunch of bin lids together from the handles, making what looked like a makeshift cart. Everyone, it seemed, loved the prospect of an actual white Christmas. Everyone except the bookies and I. The bookies' reason was for the money they would dish out to patrons that laid down their cash in June and would now line up, rubbing their hands together for the payout, me because I needed to catch a flight home.

I say a silent thank you to no one in particular, about having the hindsight to book a hotel only minutes from the airport, glad now I didn't have to make the trek through London's traffic. *He* had tried to get me to do that, pointing out that London would have more places to go, more fun to be had, but it was the one thing I insisted on; I travelled through sky to get there for him, the least he could do was travel an hour from his home. I gave him other reasons: I was only there for him, and also, if we stayed away from the city, there was less chance of being seen. That had done the trick.

There was no need for small talk with the cab driver. It was too short a journey, and my heart wasn't in it. Anyway, I had other things to preoccupy me; I was in a search for the holy grail of dolls, Miss Rainbow. A task that was proving to be a nightmare. Within no time, with no luck searching, the cab pulled up outside the departures section of Stansted Airport.

Having been there many times before, I barely glanced at the columns that splayed out like metal fingers and attached to the overhead canopy marking each doorway. Behind them, squares of glass made up the entrance of the departures terminal. Clusters of freezing smokers blocked the front of the building, getting a nicotine fix before punching their ticket and committing to being locked in to the airport for hours. I purposely sucked in some of the smoke as I passed; it was my only way of inhaling now, having given up as soon as I contemplated having children.

The doors swooshed open, and a welcome heat hit me. The brightly lit airport sprang into life. Tinny Christmas music played over the universal tannoy. Christmas trees sprinkled around the terminal and gave a little cheer to the place. People stood everywhere, in queues, in different lanes, descending on a multitude of destinations: sat on benches or sipping steaming hot drinks at the coffee docks.

A crowd huddled around one spot, the same one I gravitated to, knowing it held a huge electronic billboard and located my own hoped for destination, Cork, from the long list. It wasn't up yet. No surprise, I'd arrived early to avoid the snow, afraid if it continued it could be bad enough to halt traffic. I passed the lanes of check ins and walked to a bench away from the chaos, a bench that two people had just got up from and sat there. I was half an hour early from the start of check in, so I took out my phone and got searching for the elusive Miss Rainbow.

An hour later, I didn't panic when the flight didn't show on the board. Instead, I lay down on the now unoccupied bench and looked at the ceiling. It was impressive; a square lay in the middle of a huge panel, surrounded by a diamond-shaped window which was skyless now, but white, because of the coverage of snow. Rows and rows of triangles circumnavigated the white diamond, forming a pattern of upside down triangles next to upright ones that surrounded the diamond in a line, alternating to the opposite shape for the next row. This repeated until they formed a much bigger square. The entire ceiling continued like that; a patchwork of squares and diamonds and triangles. If I moved my head from side to side, they changed position, like stepping into one of those old 3D posters that, if you looked long enough, you would see another image pop out. It was quite hallucinating. That kept me amused for quite some time.

Two hours later though, I worried.

Three hours later, when the flight to Cork had at least appeared on the board, I began biting my nails. Every flight had the same word underneath its status. Delayed, delayed, delayed. More and more people trampled through the doors. Constantly checking the board for changes meant having to leave my seat and for every chair there were five people waiting to take my place. The noise in there was an orchestra of clicking heels, rolling wheels from luggage trolleys, wailing children, and a collection of mumblings from a thousand disgruntled passengers who were going nowhere.

The battery on my phone was only on fifty per cent; I cursed myself for not bringing a charger. I closed my eyes when I heard her voice say hello. It was like slipping into my dressing gown, comforting and reminding me of home.

'Hi mum, how is she?'

'She's grand. Missing you. How are you? Or where are you? I saw the news, they're saying the snow is bad over there.'

'Yeah, we're delayed. I'm still in Stansted. I don't know what I was thinking, mum.' My voice cracked. I looked at the ceiling panels to stop the tears.

'Shhh, honey. You weren't thinking, were you? But that's OK. Should I ask how it went?'

'No, mum, please don't.'

'Oh Peggy. When are you going to learn to stop putting a man before everything?'

'Can we talk about it later? I'm really not in the right place to go into the details.'

'Sure.'

The voice on the line sounded sad, but I couldn't think about that. I couldn't let the guilt in.

'Do you think it would upset Ellie if she spoke to me?'

'I'd leave it off. She's in the other room playing away now. Speaking to you would only remind her you're not here.'

'You're right. Give her a smooch for me.'

'Already done. Safe home, my love.'

A lump caught in my throat. 'Thanks for everything. I'd be lost without you.'

'Ah, go away out of that. Just get home, will you?'

'Working on it. I'm going to turn my phone off to save the battery but I'll ring you as soon as I know anything.'

I put away the phone and settled down. With no movement from the people huddled over the board, I could tell we weren't going nowhere.

During the fourth hour, my bladder had other plans about me staying put. I made my way past the blank space of the check in foyer and followed the signs for the bathroom, meandering through the crowd of people doing nothing but blocking the place up with their suitcases. I scowled at one girl, whose enormous case was bigger than a person. A man huddled in the corner, with a large suitcase at his feet. He was crying. When he saw me, his hands went to his head, and he burrowed his face into his knees. I had never seen a adult man cry before. Needing the bathroom urgently now, I pushed through the crowd.

Once relieved, my aim was to find another seat. This time I would try to find somewhere looking out on a billboard. On the way out, I stood aside and waited as a woman blocked the doorway with her suitcase. No matter which way she turned it, the luggage wouldn't fit through the narrow entrance. It was then I understood why there was a group outside and why, for one reason anyway, that man was crying.

Outside, the man was still there, staring at the floor. I stopped, unsure if I should approach.

I'll tell you right now something about me; I believe in good deeds and the power of intention. If I give a little to someone, if I bend myself away from my own plans or worries for a moment and help someone else having a tough time, if I help them improve their day, I've discovered it has a ripple effect and eventually the good fortune bounces back to me. In any unpleasant situation I've faced, I've tried to see the good, tried to see the way out, and if that failed and I ended up still completely miserable, I found the best way to turn the situation around was to do something for someone else. Until lately, it had worked every time.

'If anyone can't fit their suitcase in, I can mind your luggage?'

A woman next to me, done a full body scan, from my feet to my head. She didn't look impressed when she met my eyes. 'And rob us blind? You're having a laugh. Or slip something in.'

'Like what?'

'Like drugs or something.'

'You've seen my face and we are standing next to a set of security cameras and since there's no flights leaving, I've nowhere to go. Just trying to do something nice for Christmas, that's all. I don't have any luggage and in the bathroom it struck me it would be hard to leave luggage outside when you can't see it. I didn't mean to offend.'

The woman scrutinised me, then softened. 'Screw it. Sorry, this place has my nerves on edge. Go on then, I'm bursting.'

She rolled her suitcase over to me and leaned it against a marble pillar, half walking, then running to the ladies.

'Anyone else?' I said, looking in particular at the man who had stopped crying but kept his head in his hands.

'I will mate,' a scruffy-looking guy said, plonking a battered backpack bigger than himself and more suited to trekking the mountains down in front of the woman's case. He pointed a finger near my nose but took the edge off the threat with a smile. 'No robbing me now. My whole life is in there.' He rested his hands on his hips and smiled at me. 'I'm travelling around the world as soon as we can get out of here.'

'Good for you,' I said. 'Anyone else want to go? This is a last time offer. One chance and I'm gone.'

I enjoyed doing good deeds, but I wasn't a mug either. The crying man looked up, his face contorted, as if he had only just woken up from a bad dream, remembering where he was. He wiped his eyes with a violent swipe and then stood and pushed his suitcase towards me, saying nothing. With one quick nod of his head, his red-rimmed eyes looked right at me, and then he rushed off to the men's bathroom. Once another person trusted me, it opened the gates to every bladder full person trying to work out what to do, and I became inundated with requests. I didn't care. In my mind, every good deed brought me closer to my little girl, brought me closer to Ellie.

Miss Rainbow

All the seats were gone. I settled by a window on the floor and watched the snow fall thicker. Judging by the speed of it, I wouldn't leave soon.

'I love you, but you need to stop now,' I said to the snow.

Maybe I could use the delay to my advantage, I thought, turning on the phone and typing a quick search of routes from Stansted by rail. The train would still run and wouldn't have many takers going from the airport as there were no flights landing. If I travelled to only one stop and reserved the toy, maybe it was doable.

The train's first stop was 36 minutes away in Tottenham Hale, so the round trip would take at least an hour and twelve minutes, then I would have to get to the nearest toy shop, which according to my phone, was at least another twenty-minute walk. That was with no delays or wait time. It was cutting it fine. There were at least twenty toy shops in the vicinity. Would it be worth it to leave now? If I stayed and searched, I would waste more time, yet if I didn't search, I would waste the time when I got there. I could search on the train, I reasoned. Ellie's smile flashed in a memory. There was nothing for it. I would get a train.

Checking the board once more and being greeted by the same words, I made my way to the train station. I couldn't see the entrance. It was full to the brim with people.

'What's going on?' I asked a man next to me.

'Word has it they're going to close the airport. People are trying to get accommodation or get to other airports while they can.'

'But what if they're wrong?'

The man shrugged. 'Some of them think it's better to go now. When they close the airport, everything shuts down. It isn't pleasant.'

'Right. Good to know. I'd go home too if I could, but looks like I'm stuck here.'

'Sorry about that,' the man said, looking far from concerned.

'Do you think everyone will get on?'

'No way, not for one train. The crowd is too big. We won't get on till the next one, I'd say.'

'They're every fifteen minutes, yeah?'

'That's if the lines don't close. Snowfall is heavy, they might have to cancel.'

'So, if I go, I might not get back?'

The man laughed. 'Why in hell would you want to do that?'

'I'm trying to get a toy for my daughter. Thought I'd use the time I'm stuck here.'

He let out a whistle. 'You'd be taking an awful risk.'

'You're right. It's pointless having a toy if you can't get home to give it in person. Thanks for your help,' I said, moving away from the crowd.

'You know there's a massive toy shop just around the corner from the airport, right?' He called to me.

'No,' I said, swivelling back to face him.

'Yeah, big one just around the corner on the right-hand side. You won't be able to walk it though with the ice. In a car you have to go the long way around the motorway, still it would only be about a mile or so. Think it's called Toys For You. Worth a shot.'

I couldn't help it. Before I knew it, I'd given the man a hug. He looked shocked but then let out a huge laugh, starting from his belly. 'Well, that was nice.'

'Thank you,' I said. 'Merry Christmas.'

'And to you. Hope you find what you're looking for.'

'Me too,' I said, and rushed away.

The outside floor of the terminal had thickened enough to only leave a few cars waiting at the taxi rank. I leant over the passenger window.

'Do you know where Toys For You is?'

'The one round the corner?' The man asked in a thick London accent.

'That's the one.'

The man sucked in his breath, letting it run through his teeth, weighing up the pros and cons of taking me.

'If you could drop me there and wait and bring me back, I'd make it worth your while.'

The man softened with the opportunity for a longer fare. 'Get in,' he said.

'Snowed in?' He asked once I'd settled down and he'd got all the risky business of pulling out and avoiding oncoming passengers and cars out of the way.

'Looks like it for the moment, anyway. They haven't officially said anything yet. I'm hoping they're going to clear the runway and get as many planes out as possible.'

'You're taking a chance leaving, aren't you? What if they speed up check in and start boarding?'

'That's why I'm going to pay you extra if you can get there as fast as possible. I figure if that were to happen, I've got half an hour before they would even get through the queue and check everyone in.'

'Irish?' he asked.

'I am. For my sins.'

'Whereabouts? I've family in Limerick.'

'Cork, so not too far from that. Bout an hour up the road.'

I waited for him to tell me their names like most people did when you mentioned Ireland, in case I'd know them. Ireland was a small country, but not that small. He didn't. Instead, he said, 'Ah, the rebel county.'

I laughed. 'You know your stuff. There's many a Corkonian that would argue Cork is the actual capital of Ireland.'

'Not you, though?' He asked, chuckling.

'Honestly? Once I get home, I couldn't care less.'

'I take it you've a kid if you're going to a toy shop.'

'I do, a girl, a four-year-old. I've tried everywhere for one bloody toy that is proving impossible to get.'

'What is it?'

'Miss Rainbow. She has wings and rainbow hair and according to the ad can do a million different things.'

'I know the one. We got her for our granddaughter.'

'You did. Where did you get it?' I said, leaning nearer the back of his seat.

'Ah, no, we got it months ago.'

'I couldn't. She didn't want it back then. Decided this two weeks ago. You know what I don't understand, why a toy company would bombard the TV with advertising, coming on every ten minutes when there isn't a store in Europe that has them? All it leads to is misery.'

'See, I have a theory on that. There's two things going on there. For one, they probably paid for the campaign before they sold out and two, it will create such a frenzy when they get stock in, everyone will have to have it.'

'Well, if I don't get it for Ellie this Christmas, I'll make sure she doesn't want it anymore.'

He chuckled again. 'We'll see.'

Ten minutes had already passed. 'I thought it was only round the corner?'

'It is round the corner if you walked. On the road, you have to go past the motorway to get off the exit.'

'Would I have been better off walking?'

'In the snow? You could have taken your chances. It's icy in parts.

Don't worry, love, I'll get you there in a minute.'

Sure enough, the turn for the next exit appeared, and the cab driver took it. Then there was a meandering of streets where I watched people stepping on pavements with cautious, toe tapping movement, their eyes unbudging from looking down, in case of icy patches. It had been a good choice to hail a cab.

He slowed down looking for a car space and then I saw the sign. I wiggled in my seat, desperate to get out. The cab driver noticed. 'There's not much parking. How about you get out and I'll circle a few times. If I find a spot, I'll stand outside the car.'

'That would be fantastic, thanks.'

He came to a stop, and I opened the door and got out. He rolled down his window. 'You're not gonna do a runner on me, are ya?'

'Me? I've nowhere to go. I'm more worried you're going to get another fare and leave me stranded.'

'It's Christmas. I wouldn't do that.'

'Well, it's good to see you have morals. That bodes well.' I felt around in my pocket. 'I can give you a tenner if it helps?'

'Keep it. I'll trust you.' Another car beeped from behind.

'See you in a minute then,' I called as he drove away, his hand raised in a wave.

'I hope he means it,' I said under my breath as I tapped my foot along the path, feeling my way between shiny patches on the pavement.

The shop was a decent size, with aisles stacked from the floor to ceiling with toys. The heat hit me, making my body slick and sweaty under the winter clothes I was wearing. A Christmas tune boomed from the speakers, loud enough to make me cover my ears. It was full of people, so much so, it was hard to see the shelves. It wasn't the time for holding back, or feeling faint, as I needed to keep moving. I removed my scarf and unbuttoned my jacket while I squeezed past two men with hands in their pockets, shooting the breeze with each other, with no interest in shopping. You could just tell if the snow wasn't there, they would be outside instead of inside.

The first aisle was full of learning toys, I tried to go back the way I'd come in but a surge of new customers blocked my exit, all trying to do the same thing I was, so I weaved my way to the far end of the aisle. At the top were trains and planes and every other toy you could think of with wheels. The next aisle was more like it, full to the brim with baby dolls, but no matter how much I searched, there wasn't a staff member in sight to locate or even tell me if there was any Miss Rainbow left at all.

'Just one Miss Rainbow. Come on, Toys For You,' I said under my breath. Turning the corner, I hit the jackpot. The fashion doll aisle almost glowed. I ran my eyes from top to bottom, not moving on until I scanned every shelf, only stepping forward to the next section, once inspected. A crowd gathered around a staff member with a crate.

'One at a time please,' he said as strong as he could to a bunch of grabbing women.

I knew without checking it was for Miss Rainbow; only that doll got this kind of mayhem. I moved as fast as I could, joining the crowd, tiptoeing to see what was in his hand, or any of the women's hands. One lady broke through from the crowd and sure enough, there she was, Miss Rainbow with her hair in each colour of her namesake, with eyes that were almost the size of her face, sparkling in her dress. My heart quickened and a little stress left my shoulders. It had been the right choice coming here. Until the crowd dispersed and the man stood there empty-handed. I rushed towards him. The poor boy was only about sixteen. His hair was all over the place, one side of his collar stood up and he had a wounded look about him.

'Please tell me you have more Miss Rainbows' left.'

He didn't even answer, just held up the empty box. His bare arms had scratches on them.

'Any left in the stockroom?' I asked.

He shook his head and his shoulders curled in towards his chest, as if I was going to attack him.

'It's OK,' I said.

Pushing my way to the counter, I passed the queue of women clenching their Miss Rainbow dolls and didn't stop until I was in front and facing them. When I spoke, I made sure they heard me over the crowd noise and Christmas music.

'I'm looking for a Miss Rainbow doll. If any of you hand it over, I will give you fifty sterling for the trouble.'

One lady piped up. 'You having a laugh? Do you know how much these are going for on the internet? We're all in the same boat, trying to get this stupid doll.'

'If it's more money, I'm willing to up it,' I said.

Most of the women looked at the floor or at the ceiling or studied the doll, anywhere but me.

I spotted one woman had two. 'Can't you just sell me one? Why would you need two?'

'Ever hear of twins?' The woman shot back.

'Ever hear of sharing?' I said without thinking.

'Piss off,' the woman said, turning her back on me.

One woman made her purchase and bashed into me, giving me a filthy look.

Along the rest of the line, I tried the sympathy vote.

'I'm sorry, but you don't know how much this would mean to my little girl. I'm trying to get home to her.'

One woman made eye contact.

'I'm trying to get back to Ireland and, because of the snow, it's looking like I might not. It's going to ruin our Christmas. The least I could do is give her the only toy she wanted.'

The woman looked sheepish. 'Please,' I said, putting my hands together in prayer. The woman pushed back her pulled back hair, thinking. Like a dog sensing fear, I sensed a way in, an empathy coming from her. Making my eyes wider, imploring, ruthlessly trying anything I could to get through. She sighed.

'What makes you more important than any of us? Can't you see we're all in the same boat? I can't afford to give my daughter big presents, or flights away, or offer extra money like it's easy for you to do, but I drove the length of London for this doll so my little girl will get some kind of Christmas. Because I would do anything for my little one. Difference between me and you is, I wouldn't leave her ever, let alone just before Christmas. If you can't get home, you put yourself in this situation. Now, go away. I've enough problems of my own.'

The breath whooshed out of my mouth as if she'd slapped me. As the woman brushed past me, I hung my head in shame. 'I'm sorry,' I said. 'I didn't mean to insult you. Any of you. I just wanted to try anything because we've had the worst two months and wanted to show her, to prove to her, dreams can still come true.'

The woman stopped and turned back and for a moment I thought she was going to hit me, but instead of having a go, she lay a doll-less hand on my arm. 'That's why I want it for my daughter. You haven't offended me. I get why you'd try anything, but you needed to know we all have our reasons for wanting the doll. I hope you get her and I hope you get home. That will mean more to your daughter than any doll.'

'I hope so too,' I said, the tears brimming.

There were no Miss Rainbow customers left. The last two must have ducked out while I spoke to the woman. Never in my life had I felt more of a failure. At least twenty people eyed me now, waiting for my reaction or to see if I was going to hassle them, but there was no point; what I wanted was long gone. The thought of time rushed back to me. I had been longer than I'd hoped and needed to get back to the airport. The intensity of the shop became too much. The heat, the noise, the failure all stifled me and I needed air, fresh air. I rushed out of the shop to breathe again, forgetting completely about the ice and as soon as my foot hit a slippy spot, my leather high-heeled boots that seemed like the perfect choice for seduction two days ago left the ground and I landed flat down, straight on my arse.

After the searing pain dulled, it all got on top of me. So much for good deeds, or getting to the airport early, for the best of intentions, and constantly getting nowhere.

'Could this day get any worse?' I screamed at the sky.

A guy stepped over my legs, scowling at me as he passed. 'Sorry for being such an inconvenience to you by blocking your path,' I shouted, only delighted to have someone to fight with. He didn't look back.

Standing was proving difficult. The soles of my boots couldn't get any grip. Every time I tried to sit up, my legs splayed and there was nothing to grab on to, to pull myself up to standing. Even trying to scoot was futile, my hands couldn't get a stable piece of concrete. After many attempts, I gave up and sat helpless, watching the many people that passed me purposely not looking, pretending not to see. What could be more important than helping someone on the street? All it would take was a couple of seconds. And it was Christmas, the time for giving and helping others, surely it was a requirement? Ignoring someone in need was an alien concept to me, because I had spent my whole life believing you helped people when they fell, you lifted them up, and by doing that, you became a better person. And then I wept, not caring who saw. I cried for the unkindness of strangers but also for Miss Rainbow. I cried for the ridiculous situation I'd put myself in by jumping on a plane, and for the hours I'd lost in the airport that I could have used Christmas shopping or cooking or wrapping. I cried for the pain in my bum from falling and from not being able to move. Most of all, I cried for Ellie, for having such an awful mother as me.

An arm slipped under mine and I took the offer and lifted myself. My legs tried to do the splits, both going in different directions, but the arm held me strong until I was upstanding and balanced again. It was the cab driver.

'You stayed. I can't tell you how glad I am to see you,' I said, wiping my eyes.

'Works both ways. This is proving to be quite a lucrative fare.'

He hooked my arm and helped me the couple of inches to the cab. He'd landed a spot right outside the door. 'I see you dressed for the snow then,' he said, chuckling.

'Well, in fairness, I didn't think I would leave the airport.'

He opened the door of the cab for me and didn't let go of my arm until I'd settled in the seat. My eyes watered again from the gesture.

He sat back in and I saw the flicker of his eyes through the driver's mirror at my empty hands and I loved him in that moment, for his kindness in jumping to my rescue in the ice, for his silence now, for not mentioning my failure.

He pulled out. 'I checked out your flight online. Looks like they have a time up now for leaving in two hours, so at least that's something.'

One tear that threatened on the rim of my eye escaped, but this time for a different reason. 'Oh, that's everything.'

Queuing

Arriving at the airport, a little daunted and a lot more out of pocket, I rushed to the board. The cab driver was right, check in was up. I made my way to Row F, and once located, sighed with relief that the queue was still there. Doing a quick scan, there was no one in the line I recognised, which was surprising. Cork was small enough to know at least one person on the flight.

'At least I haven't messed this up,' I said.

A woman spoke from behind. 'I know. For a second there, I thought we might have to sleep here for Christmas.'

An older woman stood behind me in a coat so puffed up it made her top half double the size of the bottom of her, leaning on two suitcases, one pink, the other dark brown leather. Politeness won over my misery, and I smiled at her.

'I was cursing myself this morning for leaving it so late to come over, but I just love seeing the sights, you know?'

I nodded and turned back, pretending to check the queue but just hoping the small talk was over. Sore and fragile after the toy shop, I craved some quiet. Still, the woman continued.

'Every year we used to come. Even when we were courting, we flew over to see the lights in the West End.' She giggled like she was younger, like she was remembering something that made her feel young. I moved nearer. 'It became a tradition. It wasn't Christmas unless we got away and walking down those streets turned into my favourite part of it all. We loved it so much, it was the only place my Arthur could think of to propose, got down on one knee, all lit up by the lights behind it glowed around him and made him look like he shone, like he was some god or something.'

This time I gave in to the conversation. 'Like a halo.'

'Then the children came along and we made a big thing of bringing them. It was different when they were small. More stressful but more magical, too. We loved it. Lived for it really, all year long we'd save to make it happen. And then they got older and didn't want to go, they'd complain, saying they wanted to stay with their friends or had other things planned so we sent them to their grandparents and got used to it being us two again, we saw it as our cheeky getaway.'

The woman laughed and her wrinkled creases didn't take away from eyes that were bright blue.

'That's lovely.'

She dropped her smile. 'This was the first year I wondered if I should still go. I wasn't going to. The kids all tried to make me stay, but I felt I owed him to come one more time, you know? Still, my son insisted he join me and I'm glad I came. Christmas is all about traditions, and I couldn't break the most important one.'

'I'm so sorry,' I said, and found I meant it.

Her smile left completely. 'It was my last time, though. This trip just wasn't the same without him. Everything was different. The place felt threatening, hostile, even with my son beside me I was scared out of my wits! The same lights that shone so bright, looked tacky. We used to say it was like coming home, but this time I felt nothing. Yet it was the same place, with the same atmosphere, and the West End hadn't changed at all. I came all this way to realise it wasn't the trip that made Christmas special but him, he made it special.'

'Sounds to me like he loved you very much.'

She dabbed at her eyes with a tissue. 'Have you a husband?'

A young man came up beside her and put his hands over both suitcase handles, saving me from the question. 'Thanks Mum,' he said, taking them from her while smiling at me.

'Well, let's hope we can get home soon and turn our attention to celebrating Christmas.'

'Here's hoping,' she said.

I nodded my goodbyes to them both and turned to face the front again, glad of the distraction. This day was exhausting. The queue shuffled nearer and a quick head count told me there were about ten ahead. The fourth head away was shuffling more than the others and was making a racket. Every time he needed to go further in the queue, he kicked his bag. He had a jerky way of walking and he wouldn't stand still, instead he rolled on his heels, or wobbled from side to side. Drunk.

The man in front of me spoke in hushed tones into his phone, but I still caught bits of the conversation.

'How long have I got?'

The back of his head retreated until his skull was almost touching his back.

'I don't know if I can get there in time. I'm trying my best, I promise.' His voice ended in a strangled sob, like a baby that has cried so long their breath replaces their voice, when there's no sound left to dispense.

Another man was making a scene at the desk, and he wasn't even trying to keep his voice down. He banged on the counter.

'I need to leave now.'

It was the man that had been crying by the bathroom earlier.

'It's not just you getting on the flight, sir. We have to ensure all passengers get on board.'

'But if you hurried it up, we could all be on board within thirty minutes. What are we waiting for?'

The woman looked at the ceiling and took more than a moment before reacting, as if she was trying to calm herself. When she spoke, she enunciated her words slowly and in the same tone as if talking to a child. 'There are protocols, sir. We have to allow a certain amount of time for passengers to get to the plane, and there are safety checks that have to be carried out before we leave.'

'But the plane has been sitting there for hours,' he said at the top of his voice, waving his arms in the air. He gesticulated wildly, pointing at the glass windows.

The woman crossed her arms. 'Sir, please, if you don't calm down, we will have to ban you from the flight altogether. We can't have these disruptions on the plane.'

The man covered his face with his hands and took a few breaths. 'I'm sorry. Look,' he said, pointing to his chest. 'I'm calm.' He pointed to the glass again. 'My point is the snow is only going to get worse. We have a small window of time where the runway clears after the snow eases up. I will carry anyone who can't walk if it means the plane takes off quicker. I'm just under pressure. It's a life or death situation and what I'm trying to say is if there is anything I can do to speed that up, I will.'

The woman uncrossed her arms and softened. 'Sir, I understand your concern. We are doing our very best to get everyone out on the flight, but it has to be done safely, which means using a queuing system for planes. You can't just take off at an airport, you know? We have a time slot and if you hurry and don't delay the queue any longer, we will stick to it.'

The man conceded, and the rest of the conversation went unheard. The exchange left a shuffling unrest in the crowd though, with many showing signs of agitation. A couple near the back sounded like they were having an argument, but it was a scene a few passengers in front that was causing the most noise. A woman struggled with two screaming children, who were pulling each arm as she tried to move up. She looked like one of those toys whose arms stretched. The poor woman. We were all desperate to get home and sick of waiting, but at least we were doing it without having to keep children occupied.

Although my last good deed hadn't worked, here was another opportunity to swing things my way. The old woman behind was deep in conversation with her son, so I left them alone. I knew she wouldn't make a fuss if I stepped out of the line, so I tapped the man in front of me. He turned around and for a moment I regretted it; the man looked shook, with red rings around his eyes and a face so pale you could almost see through it.

'What?' he said sharply, still holding his phone.

'I'm so sorry. I didn't think you were still on a phone call.'

He looked at his phone as if it was something he was only noticing for the first time. 'I'm not,' he said.

'I just wanted to offer that lady with the kids something, but I don't want to lose my place. I was just hoping you'd vouch for me in case anyone in front thinks I'm skipping.'

He shrugged in acceptance, running his hand through his neck long hair. It was nice hair, dark with flecks of grey. Hair that said he'd lived, survived even. I pushed away the thought, replaced it with another, an image, of me waking up naked this morning, of feeling more alone than ever, of a guilty woman on her knees scrambling for her clothes in the dark. Another man was not what I needed now.

The woman looked like she was going to burst into tears. A boy with the same blond curls as her lay on the ground and pulled her with such force it slanted her body sideways. He was wearing a Christmas jumper with an elf on it, giving me an idea. The girl, about the same age as the boy, still blonde but with straight hair, was wailing at the top of her lungs. They were still three from the top of the queue.

'I hear we have two very special people trying to go to Cork for Christmas.'

The two children were so shocked by the interruption they stopped crying and looked at me suspiciously.

'I'm sorry,' the woman said, about to apologise further.

'No need,' I said, raising my hand to stop her. 'I'm here to let you know I'm Santa's representative for the airport and I just wanted to say how much I think these guys are doing such a great job so far.'

The boy dropped the woman's hand and lay still on the floor.

'Now, I know airports can be really boring and you've had to wait such a long time but you have to remember, there's only a very short amount of time left until it's Christmas and there's people like me,' I whispered the next bit, 'and of course the elves, who told me to let you know they are hiding and watching all over the place.'

I saluted at a spot over their shoulder.

'You saw them?' The girl asked, looking around.

'Did you not see them?' I asked her, acting shocked.

The boy got to his feet and joined the girl, shaking his head. 'We have an elf at home and we haven't been able to see if he moved.'

'But sure, there's no point anyway,' I said, shaking my head. 'He won't be there. It's your elf's job to watch your behaviour, so he has to go where you go or if he can't get near enough, he appoints helpers like me. What's your elf's name?'

'Duster,' they said in unison.

'Yep, I know Duster,' I said, nodding with authority and tapping my chin for effect. 'I was wondering if he was yours. I met him a second ago, going for a spin in the revolving luggage thingy. He told me he's been watching you and you were both in line to have a wonderful Christmas, but he's worried that you're going to mess up all your good work by being bored waiting for this stupid flight. He couldn't come up to you and tell you himself because that would ruin the magic, so that's where I come in.'

'You speak to elves?' the boy asked.

'Not usually,' I said, leaning into him, 'but he appointed me human ambassador and well, I couldn't refuse because I want you to have the best Christmas ever.'

I winked at the grateful mum and squatted down to the kids' level; they leaned into me to hear more. 'Duster told me why we have to wait so long. Santa needs the runway cleared so he can see where to land Christmas Eve, so the good people in the airport are trying to beat the snow and clear it for them. But as it's so boring, we wanted to give you something to make it better.'

I reached into my bag and pulled out two cellophane wrapped flat boxes. 'Who likes to colour?'

They both threw their hands in the air. 'Well, that's good because I have two packs of colouring books here for you.'

I handed them a colouring book each, both with a picture of an elf on the front. 'It's a story as well. You have to help your elf find his way home for Christmas.'

'But how can we help him if *we* can't get home?' The girl said in a quiet voice.

'You'll get home. You just have to believe. Don't you know Christmas is the time for miracles?'

'Like baby Jesus?' The boy asked.

'Just like baby Jesus,' I said, nodding. 'Now I'm going to go back to my spot in the queue. Keep an eye out for Duster, but remember, having patience and being good for your mammy is going to bring the best Christmas ever.'

'OK,' they said, putting on their 'I'm as good as gold faces'. An expression I'd seen many times from Ellie.

'Happy Christmas,' I called.

The woman tapped the kids on the head. 'Say thank you guys.'

'Thank you,' they said together, already tearing open their packs. 'Look what we got, mum,' the boy said.

'I know. How lucky are ye?'

On the way back to my spot, no one questioned me, so I figured they had just watched. The man stepped back to let me pass. His skin was less pale, and some warmth had flushed his cheeks, taking away his haunted look. 'That was really kind what you just did for that woman.'

I shrugged. 'Travelling with kids is hard at the best of times, let alone stuck in a snowstorm just before Christmas. If they think I'm watching them, they might make life a little easier for their mother.'

'Well, thank you from a guy who wanted to keep his hearing and his nerves.'

'There's that, too. After hearing my own crying child for so long, whenever I hear someone else's, my first thought is alarm that it might be mine and the second is an urge to fix it.'

'A mother's affliction,' he said, nodding in understanding at first, but then his eyes glossed over and he went to turn away from me.

'I think babies make a heart grow bigger, but because of that, there is more pressure on the organ. There's too much blood to pump around, and the bigger it gets, the closer it is to your chest bone, giving a tightness there that doesn't go away. I've never felt fear like it until my daughter was born. Or stress.'

He broke out in a smile, and as he did, all his features softened. 'I hear you. You have one child?'

'Yeah, a four-year-old.'

He nodded and shuffled nearer in the queue, then turned back, looking confused. 'Why did you have two colouring pads?'

'I bought them for my daughter and my sister's children. There's another two in my bag, so if we hear any more screaming kids on the flight, you know who's getting them.'

'I like your style,' he said, chuckling. It was a warm laugh, making me laugh, too.

Another staff member opened up the desk beside the woman and the crowd in front split in half. The woman and two kids were now being checked in.

'Have you children?'

'I do. I'm separated from their mother, but I see them as much as I can.'

'Oh, sorry,' I said.

'It's amicable, thank god. We split up about ten years ago, so the pain isn't raw anymore. Four years ago, my job needed me to move to London. The kids wanted to stay in Cork, so I made a deal that I would work a four-day week and fly back every Thursday to Sunday so we could share custody. The older they get, the more they like coming over to London. I became the cool dad.' He used that laugh again. 'It's Cork for Christmas this year, so I'll stay with them.'

'You spend it together?'

'Course, that's the least we can do for the kids. Like I said, it was amicable, so it makes it easier.'

'Was it like that from the start, or did time heal all? I'm sorry, you don't have to tell me if it's too much.'

'No, you're fine. The day I'm having, I need something to distract me. It was like that from the start. We got together very young, we were both only fifteen. You know that old cliche of middle age crisis? Well, my wife just woke up one day as she neared thirty and said she didn't want to be married anymore. We'd had the kids young too, and she'd given everything to her family, and the time had come when they were getting older that she wanted to go out and live a little, put herself first for once. I couldn't argue with that. She had been pregnant right after our exams, even at her debs she couldn't drink. I still got to go to college while she stayed at home minding the baby. Four kids later, she'd had enough of being the stay at home mum.' He raked a hand through that nice hair. 'Still though, her decision kind of blindsided me at the time because if she'd told me she felt that way, if she'd wanted to stay with me and do all those things, I would have supported her. It took some time to understand. I'd never felt like I missed out on all that going out, but I accepted her decision. She said she couldn't change unless we separated because she only knew one way to be around me. We had become more like flatmates and I don't know why I'm offloading all this to you, sorry.'

'You're not. I'm pushing you for information. It's making the queue seem shorter, anyway.'

It was true; the queue had reduced to just one in front of him.

'Cool,' he said, even though he looked embarrassed.

'So, you're going home to Cork to see your kids?'

He hesitated. 'That's one reason. They range from twenty down to thirteen, so most of them will have their own plans, but if I'm lucky, the older ones will have a pint with their old man and the teenager might allow me to take him somewhere. We'll have Christmas day together, which is the main thing. There's another reason I need to get home though.'

The old woman behind tapped me. 'Sorry, I know you're having a good chat, but could you tell him to move up? We want to get home this side of Christmas,' she said with a wry smile.

'Sorry,' we both said, then laughed. The man was, in fact, next. I gestured with my hand for him to move. 'The floor is yours, sir.'

'So, it is. I'm Niall,' he said.

'Peggy.'

'See you,' he said.

'See you.'

I busied myself getting my passport and tickets out of my bag and tried to stop the goofy smile that had plastered on my face. I needed to focus and not get distracted by good-looking men. That was what had got me into this situation. What mattered was getting back to my girl. Soon, I would be home and Ellie would be in my arms again. This was still going to be a good Christmas, I was sure of it. All I had to do was get on that flight.

Stuffed

The check in was quick, seeing as I had no luggage. On my way out, I couldn't help to look back at Niall, but he was still showing his passport, so I moved on. I wanted to get to the duty free to see if there was anything I could pick up that would make up for the colouring books I'd given away. To make up for not being there.

Now that I had some news, I rang my mother again. The phone picked up on the first ring.

'Hello?'

'Hi mum, how is she?'

'She's grand. Are you stranded there?'

'Still stuck in Stansted, but I've checked in and they've given us a departure time for two. I'm going to need you to mind her for longer and mum could you also pick up the turkey from Brosnan's or else they'll be nothing for dinner tomorrow?'

'Course I will. Love, don't worry about us. Just get yourself home.'

There was a bang, followed by a gasp from my mother. Ellie had taken a tumble, or worse.

'Is she OK? Mum?'

I heard wailing and my stomach lurched. I wanted to time travel, to leap into the phone and transport myself to Cork.

'Peggy, I have to go. She's hurt her leg. Don't worry, she's fine, I just need to go to her, OK?'

The phone went dead before I could answer and right then I felt like the worst mother in the world. It should have been me picking up Ellie from the ground. Me sticking on the plaster and kissing her better. And I wasn't there. And for what? All for a lay at a layover.

At the duty free, I bought enough chocolate to keep Ellie up all night on Christmas Eve, but figured I could give her some as a begging forgiveness present and slip the rest under the tree. My phone beeped, and I opened a picture of a smiling Ellie waving and instead of reassuring me, I felt worse. I needed to get home.

Eager to get to the boarding gate as soon as possible, I followed the signs. Stansted Airport was big, way bigger than Cork airport, and could mean a long walk depending on which gate you were at. I wanted to get there straight away, not that it would speed up the journey, but to help my growing anxiety by being where I should be in plenty of time.

The boarding gate area was one huge rectangle with two opposite walls of glass. Dotted along those walls were small desks surrounded by chairs for the appointed passengers, with planes parked beyond, like waiting cabs. On seeing the designated aircraft for Cork, I almost wept at its realness, the plane touchable beyond the pane.

Our check in time came and went. I couldn't see Niall. Other than people, all that was in the room were a few vending machines and bathrooms. Without luggage and only the small carry on allowed, people were getting bored and agitated. Minutes turned slowly into hours and nobody told us anything, with no electronic billboards. I sat facing my plane and watched no one enter or come out of the aircraft, the snowfall soft but continuous and all the while tried to calm my speeding heart. I counted thirty people along the row I sat on with their head craned, watching or playing with their phones. What would they do if their batteries ran out? That's when the trouble would start. My own was on dodgy territory, run down to the last quarter. There had been ports on the chairs in the airport but with no plug, were worthless. Waiting is exhausting. More and more people joined the crowd, and a frustrated energy grew. We were being stuffed into a room and the air was growing thin.

Passengers swarmed or jumped in the way of any staff member that dared venture down and fired them with questions, some, in my opinion, were too much for one person to answer, almost sounding philosophical.

'Why are we here?'

'How long are you going to keep us here?'

One man sounded desperate. 'Are ye going to cancel the flights? If I leave, I can catch a flight to Heathrow, but I would have to go now.'

'Sir, if you leave before we cancel the flight, we won't compensate you.'

'But if you delay on cancelling, I'll miss both flights and you'll have to put me up somewhere costing you more money.'

The woman arched her brow at him but said nothing. Her look said it all. If they cancelled the flight, they weren't putting anyone up.

'This is ridiculous,' the man said, raising his voice.

'Sir, we can't tell you what we don't know. If you'd prefer to leave and take your chances in Heathrow, you are welcome, but just remember you are in the boarding area, so we are planning to send you on your way. Also, if you have any luggage, it is loaded on the plane or on the way to by now, which means you would have to wait for it to be taken off, and so would everyone else on your flight, which is pretty lousy if you ask me.'

The man looked sheepish. 'Fine,' he said, defeated.

'None of us wants this, OK? The airport wants everyone to get home for Christmas. We are trying our best, sir. Now, parts of the runway are clear, so we should call on you soon.'

She scurried off before anyone else could affront her. The people kept on piling in. We were like matches in a box, all that was needed was someone to light us up. We were slaves to the weather, passengers waiting for our turn at a trip to the sky. There was nowhere we could escape to. The smokers were getting edgier and edgier, with nowhere to slip out and have a sneaky puff. Vape sticks were sucked on all around me, and no one challenged them either, despite the signs stating they were forbidden. There was a sense of foreboding, as the sky darkened and my hope faded.

We were trapped.

Moving

A flight attendant appeared just as I was about to give up all hope. Her ironed, polished appearance made me feel grubbier, yet I was never so happy to see anyone in my whole life. She busied doing god knows what, getting the desk ready, and I prayed it would be our gate she was opening. The uniform was promising; it was green and white, which were the colours of a certain airline I was travelling on.

After five hours of waiting, we were moving. The gate opened, and another queue formed, a queue that I leapt to stand in. I stopped myself from crying, for the relief was palpable in our part of the room because we were the lucky ones being called. The ones still sitting threw us envious glares that didn't offend. I understood I was lucky and, if it had been me sat there instead, I would have stepped over every one of those in line, if it meant I took their place.

As slow as the day had gone, the flight attendants were flying through the ticket inspection now. They were in a rush. With only a quick glance, they nodded me through; I had to stop from hugging the girl, this miracle worker, this giver of hope, this enabler, reuniting me with my loved ones. Instead of gushing at her, I gave her a watery smile and moved on, desperate to get to my destination. After being immobile for so long, my legs felt clunky. The passengers walked as if they were on fast forward, walking at a faster speed than what could be classed as brisk. That's when I understood, we all were thinking the same thing; we needed to get on the plane to believe it, to believe that we were getting home.

I resisted the urge to kiss the airplane, but vaulted the metal stairs with my heart pressing on my chest with the excitement. The hostess greeted me and directed me to my numbered seat and as I sat at my appointed window, I couldn't recall being happier in a very long time. I closed my eyes and breathed. I was going home. All was well.

As the plane filled, I kept my eyes shut. They were sore and tired, but also there was an element of not wanting to jinx anything, like a child waiting for a present to be revealed, I didn't want to open my eyes until we were ready to go, until nothing could stop us.

'We meet again,' I heard.

There Niall was. 'Looks like they sat us next to each other.'

I shuffled up even though it wouldn't make any more space in the allocated seats, more to look accommodating than anything else.

'No offence, but they could have offered me a seat next to a serial killer for this flight and I would have still taken it.'

He chuckled, a head back, open-mouthed laugh I was learning to expect from him. 'No offence taken. I would have done the same. It feels good to be going home.'

'You still think of it as home, even though you're based in London?'

He shrugged. 'Home is where you're happiest.'

'You don't like London?'

'I do. It's just my family lives in Cork. It's times like this you just want to be five minutes away. Where you can just get in the car and see them. I had no choice to leave. The company I work for closed their Cork branch, so if I wanted to keep my job, there was no choice but to relocate. In some ways, it worked out. It meant a promotion and way more money, but at the start, without my kids, the loneliness, god, it left me breathless. The first night without them, I didn't think I'd make it to the morning. I worried they would blame me for leaving, that they would hate me or grow distant. And it does change things. I can't be there if one of them is in trouble. They can't knock on my door for advice. Sure, I'm only a phone call away, still though, it's never the same as breathing in the same air as them, as being able to give them a hug. It's times like this you notice. All the money in the world can't help you get home in a snowstorm when you need to.'

He stopped, creased up his eyes. 'Why is it every time I see you, I have a desire to tell you everything about me?'

'I have that type of face. Strangers always feel the need to tell me their stories.' The shock on his face made me laugh. 'I'm joking. Talking makes life interesting, and the journey passes quicker.'

'Well, no offence to you this time, but I'll be glad the quicker this journey ends. I need to get home.'

'Yeah, me too. Do you mind if I just make a quick call to let them know before we have to turn them off?'

'Good idea,' he said, half standing to fish his phone from his pocket. The last of the passengers were filtering through, so we didn't have long. Soon, my phone battery wouldn't matter. After the flight, it was back home to chargers and daughters and mothers and a million to do lists. The phone rang and rang and no one answered. It was coming up to six. My mother would be in the kitchen fixing something to eat for Ellie, with some music blaring or sitting cuddled up together, watching a movie. My heart stabbed at not being able to hear her voice now, to not hear her reaction. The message prompt beeped.

'Guess where I am? I'm on the runway, taking off any minute. I have to turn my phone off so see ye on the other side. Love ye.'

Niall was on the phone still, his head hung almost to his chin. I gave him as much privacy as I could in that small space by looking out the window. I needed to gather myself, anyway. Even if they didn't hear the message, they would know soon enough that I had kept my promise. Two hours at most. I pictured walking in my front door, scooping Ellie into my arms and taking a breath of her hair, that sweet smell of her, the epitome of home, the only place I ever wanted to be. Even now I could imagine her face next to mine, the softest skin against my cheek, knowing everything else could fall away and disintegrate, and I would still have everything I needed.

The attendants made their checks, and I kept calm, staring out the window. I wasn't in the mood for small talk anymore. The night had come upon us and outside the plane was in darkness, with only the clear path illuminated by the buildings in the distance. The safety checks and the exit sign procedure took forever, and I felt like snapping at them to hurry, to just get us up in the air, but I didn't look away from the window. My sole concern was for movement, for leaving the ground. We could worry about the journey once up there. I closed my eyes for a second, wishing and praying for them all to settle, needing the assurance of motion.

And then we were moving, slow but unbumpy, towards the runway. A few passengers whooped and others clapped. There were no crying children, no whining noises because nobody was upset to leave. Every person in my line of view, were leaning toward the seat ahead of them, as if willing the plane forwards. If I thought scooting in my seat would make the plane go faster and gain momentum, if there was anything at all I could do to give it more power, I would have. The excitement built until it was a real, living thing. You could hear it in the silence, the plane almost eerily quiet as everyone took the moment in. It was actually happening, after the worry of the morning, after thinking we were stuck there, we were on our way home and wanting to share the happiness with someone, I smiled at Niall who grabbed my hand and squeezed it once. All the hassle, all the waiting, was worth it to fly home. Gratitude brimmed out of me, for the plane, for the flight, for the attendants and the pilot, for giving me my dream to see my daughter.

We sped up from a crawl to steady.

A fleck of snow floated past the window, waltzing in the air, the particle struck me as a lone and beautiful thing, as it drifted in the black sky until it made its last wrong move and splat against the window, becoming an icy spot on the pane. I placed my finger over it on the double glazed glass, following it down as it slid away. We were so lucky. The lights in the plane turned off and the clear path became light lined runway. Within seconds, we would start getting faster, start on our ascent. My hands made fists in my lap, ready for the surge.

Within seconds, the snowfall thickened; the flecks became a flurry that turned into a blizzard. The passengers stayed silent, all transfixed by the onslaught of snow beating against the windows. A feeling deep in my stomach lurched and dropped lower, reaching the pit of me. The wind picked up with such force the plane swayed. I saw right then what would happen next. They would make us get out of the plane. Sure, they would hum and deliberate, but that amount of snowfall, in such a short time, had already covered the cleared runway. The pilot would apologise through the tannoy, his voice cracking from the static and he would say something about the conditions being too dangerous to fly but would end his announcement on a cheerful note, something concocted to stop the mass panic that was building, something like, 'your safety is paramount to us. Don't worry, as soon as the snow clears, we will get you home.' They would ask us to take our bags and the door of the aircraft would open and the flight attendants would say goodbye and wish us well, only making the briefest of eye contact because what could they say? They didn't have the answers, and had homes to go to just like us. I knew before they said a word that we would have to trudge through the already deep snow where once inside, they would make us wait for our luggage and send us back to the same terminal we had started in but this time there was no more hope of flying that night and through all that, my main thought would be of Ellie and how distraught she would be when I didn't walk through that door like I promised her. The premonition came true, exactly as I imagined and as I left my seat, as I trudged, as I stood in the same terminal, I was haunted by time. A few seconds was all it would have taken. If we had only left a minute earlier, if the flight attendants were quicker with their safety checks, or if the passengers were faster getting into the seats, we would have already been up in that sky.

Stuck

The woman in departures held her clipboard as a weapon and I didn't blame her, the crowd were baiting for blood and made for an intimidating group. Even so, she looked bored, as if a snowstorm was an everyday thing, something she had become complacent about.

Some passengers headed straight for the bar from departures, making the most of the opportunity, starting their festivities early, or just wanting to drown in their sorrows. Some had trailed off in search of food or water and even though my stomach was talking to me, growling at me now, I had made my way straight to the check-ins. Niall matched my steps. Without a word, we had become companions and I was glad of the company. We waited for the woman to speak.

'You need to queue up to see if you can get on the next available flight out of here.'

'Don't we all just transfer over to the next flight, since the plane is sitting there empty?' A drained looking woman asked.

'That's not the way it works. Your flight should have left. We've missed that time slot now and the airline has officially cancelled your flight. The next flight scheduled was when the plane returned and that one has its own passengers already booked. They get the priority.' She checked her clipboard, flicking to the next page. 'It isn't a full flight, so there will be some seats, and then some people might not show because of the weather. It's booked on a first come, first serve basis, so I suggest getting in line. The desk closes in half an hour, so if I were you lot, I'd get moving.'

'What happens if the weather gets worse?'

'Then the passengers roll over and over until you either can get on one or give up.'

I let out a groan.

'But what if we don't all get through now?' A man asked.

She shrugged. 'We'll deal with all that after. I wouldn't be worrying about the what ifs if I were you, but about getting over there.' She nodded to the line, 'as some are trying to beat you to it. For now, we are going on the assumption the next flight first thing in the morning is going ahead, so, go on, time's a wasting,' she said, ushering us away from her and pointing to the desk.

The old woman and her son were at the counter, and the mother and kids I had threatened with the elves were behind them. First off the plane, the flight attendants gave the elderly and children priority, and I didn't begrudge them. Yet, despite the conversations I'd had with them both earlier, if they offered me their ticket, I would have snatched it from them without hesitation because a ticket in their hand was one less for me. The clock ticked, and the minutes dragged.

'How long does it take to book a person in?' Niall said, trying to make light of the situation.

'We won't get there, will we?' I asked.

He shook his head. 'If they continue at this speed, I don't think so.'

'I have to get home.'

'I do too.'

'How good are you at swimming?'

'In this cold?' he laughed.

We shuffled along, until there was only two in front of me, even though we had got to the line together, Niall, had stood behind me without speaking, and I had just nodded at him, knowing that decision may cost him a spot. The guy in front was the same guy that had kicked off at the first check in and the closer we got to the counter, the more agitated he looked. As the clock struck the hour, the lights turned off, and I waited for him to lose it.

'That's it, guys,' the attendant said, raising her arms in the air as if she was blameless.

She came around the counter, expecting the onslaught she received.

'Are you just going to leave us here?' The guy said, more together than I expected.

'What happens to us now?' The man in front of him asked.

'Are we going to get hotel rooms?' A woman from somewhere behind Niall shouted.

The woman took a deep breath, expelling it out slowly and spreading her arms out for effect. When she spoke, she addressed the crowd loudly.

'All hotel rooms are booked out at the airport. The trains have closed as the snowfall is too thick. It is a waste of time trying to get to London, as everything has gone on shutdown.'

'How will we eat? Where will we sleep?'

'There are some shops at the airport.' She checked her watch, knowing full well it was only just after eight. 'Most of them are already closed, but the food court stays open until half past.'

'So what then? You can't leave us like this. Doesn't the airport have to stay open?' I asked.

She shook her head. 'No, sorry. Everything will close. The check-in desk will open again at five in the morning, and as already explained, the flights will open on a first come, first serve basis so I would suggest going away, getting food or whatever supplies that are needed and hurrying back and forming a queue. It will be the difference between getting on a flight or not.'

Panic crept up my skin. I couldn't stay here. In a moment of weakness, I took out my phone and as soon as it powered on, I text him.

Stuck in Stansted for the night. Save me!

The phone beeped within seconds.

Want me to shovel you out?

I laughed then, but the laugh came out high and desperate. It was the truth. Even he couldn't do anything for me. I had just embarrassed myself for nothing.

Yet the phone beeped again.

Roads are closed into Stansted. I could get some of the way but you might have to walk to the car. Meant to be bad out there. They're saying on the news, once the snow stops, the airport is going to do their best to get everyone home. You can always come to mine for Christmas if not. Glad you text, we didn't get to speak this morning.

Speaking was the last thing I wanted to do.

I'll stay here. Thanks though.

'Looks like I'm not eating then,' said the guy first in line for the desk. Hostile guy between eyed him up.

'Can you tell us are there even seats left on the next one or are we wasting our time?' Niall asked, sweeping a hand through his hair.

She looked around, checking if there were any staff around. 'There are two seats left.' She whispered the next bit, 'So if I were you, I would stay put.'

Facing sleep on a hard floor while in a queue was not appealing. I fought back the tears.

'I know we've only just met, but looks like we're spending the night together,' I said to Niall.

Niall covered his face with his hands. At first, it looked like he was trying to wipe away his exhaustion, but when I saw his shoulders rocking, I realised he was crying.

'Come here,' I said, and even though he didn't hug me back and his hands stayed where they were, he leaned in. I held him until his body loosened in mine. After he stopped, his chest deflated, and he said, 'I have to get home.'

'I know Niall.'

'You don't,' he said, looking up at me, his eyes childlike, full of vulnerability.

'Niall, we will get home. We're nearly there.'

'But it will be too late.'

He didn't look at me anymore; instead, he went away somewhere else, his mind on another time with different people.

I checked my watch. It was ten past. I placed my hand on his, and he moved. He stared down at it but said nothing. 'Niall, I'm going to go to the food court and get us some food. You need to eat. Is there anything you want?'

He stared down at my hand but didn't speak.

'I'll chose so. I won't be long. If you need the bathroom or need to get something after, I'll hold your spot. OK?'

He continued to stare, but I caught a slight tip of his head, enough movement to reassure me he wouldn't get up and leave the queue so we'd both lose our place. Just in case, I needed more back up. I stood in front of the two before me, my rivals now.

'I know the two of you are in for a long night, so I'm going to the food court and thought you might want something?'

The man who had argued at the counter still looked angry. 'How is that fair? We can't move yet you can go off shopping?'

'Look, if you think you won't need the toilet for the night or move once from this queue, then fine, I won't go. Or you can stop being an arsehole and I can get us all sandwiches. Your choice.'

He weighed up what I said while he stubbed the floor with his foot. 'Fine,' he said.

The first man smiled up at me. 'I'd kill for a cup of tea.'

'Any allergies?'

The two of them shook their head.

'Away I go so.'

The food court shelves were still well stocked, considering the whole airport faced a night on its floor. Maybe they had all already eaten, or maybe the store stocked up again, or maybe the passengers hadn't been told about the place. I thought about how long the queue was back in that line, about good deeds, about how if you were alone in the airport, your options became very limited, or about the people on a budget that hadn't allowed for this to happen. The airline had offered no help, and, in shock, we hadn't thought of asking. In our hesitation, they had shut up shop in minutes and ran.

In the aisle for the food court, the man who had stood on the brink of leaving and asked if he could go to Heathrow when there was still an option now eyed an egg and cress sandwich. He took a gamble and stayed and found he had for nothing. We were all losers.

I took a basket and grabbed a dozen sandwiches and a dozen rolls, leaving enough to not empty the shelves. I grabbed some cakes and crisps and chocolate bars. Comfort food would get us through the night. The staff were getting ready to close, taking in signs from outside, one check-out girl was counting money, anticipating they might need a quick exit I gathered, because once the passengers realised there was nowhere else open, they would descent on this place and there would be no getting them out for hours. As soon as that time struck half past, they were pulling down those shutters.

I lingered over the wines and wondered if I was brave enough to drink in an airport on my own. The coffee cardboard trays determined how many cups I could carry. They had ones that fit six, so that was what I would buy. I filled up half tea and half coffee, depositing plenty of sugar and enough little cartons of milk to live off them alone for the night. I added napkins and little wipes and then grabbed waters and fizzy drinks.

As I handed over my credit card, I made a silent thank you for being able to do that, for having money in my account to make that slight gesture for people without it breaking me. Money did that. It paved opportunity and gave me choices and right then, I never appreciated it more.

Laden down with two massive plastic bags and trying not to scald myself with the hot cups, I was glad the walk wasn't too far. The first thing I did was dole out the drinks, placing a tea in the hands of the first man.

'You are a lifesaver, you know that?' He said.

'I'll give you some milk and sugar in a sec. Tea or coffee?' I said to the angry man, who had lost some of the hostility and instead looked crestfallen.

'I don't have cash on me.'

'My treat. What's your preference?'

'Coffee please.'

I placed a tea down next to him in my spot.

'Niall, will you have something? Would you prefer tea or coffee?'

He looked at me then, and when he found my face, his eyes focused again. 'Coffee, please,' he said.

I walked further down the line. Next up was a guy about twenty and behind him a girl about the same age. 'I've a tea and a coffee here if anyone fancies it?'

They snapped them up in seconds. I proceeded down the line, handing out sandwiches and rolls. Any kids in the queue got a bar or a cake and seeing their faces light up made me put my hand in my pocket and pinch my skin to stop the tears from coming. No kid should have to face a night of what we were facing. Some were honest and admitted they had eaten, but all were glad of the offer. I found that gesture, the offer to help, softened them. When bad things happen, kindness always makes the difference.

Back in the queue, I sat on the floor and sipped my tea in silence. The smiles of the children had taken away my appetite and made me think of Ellie. After gathering my resolve, I turned my phone back on. A voice message flashed up. A cheery Ellie spoke to me, 'See you soon mummy'

I cried then, and didn't care who saw, 'how can I ring her and tell her I won't be home?' I wailed.

Niall stayed silent. He had changed since leaving the plane, yet as I cried, it shook him out of his trance, straightening his back. He looked as if he'd only woken up and gave me a hopeless, understanding straight lipped smile. The man on the other side of me, angry guy as I had now labelled him, looked like he was going to say something but thought better of it.

I dialled the number.

My mother answered, breathless. 'Hello, are you at the airport? We've been waiting up for you.'

If you could have put me in front of a mirror and labelled all of my mistakes in front of me, I would have felt the same way: I was the worst mother in the world.

'I'm so sorry, Mum,' I said, my voice cracking.

'Oh no,' she said, her voice hushed, already trying to shield my daughter. A job I had made her need to do, a job I should do, not her. 'What happened?'

'They made us get off the flight. We were on the runway and the snow fell again. It was too heavy.'

'Well, it's better that you didn't fly then. We want you home alive. It doesn't matter if it's tomorrow.'

My mother always knew how to see the positive in every situation.

'Mum, I'm sorry, she's going to be distraught.'

There was a pause on the line, then my mother spoke in loud, exaggerated, hushed tones. 'A secret mission for Santa, you say? Course Ellie will understand. She knows how important it is for everyone to get their presents, don't you, Ellie?'

The phone muffled, and I heard Ellie's sweet voice, high pitched yet soft, a child's innocent tone, full of wonder but sad too, 'Is mummy not coming home?' and my mother's quick explanation, some of which I couldn't decipher, just hearing tidbits like: Santa, helping, mission.

And then my girl was on the line. 'Hi mummy,' she said, not hiding the disappointment.

'Honey, I'm so sorry I can't be there tonight, but if you're a good girl for Nana, I will give you an extra big present.'

'Miss Rainbow?' she asked.

'You never know,' I said, kicking myself. That damn doll. 'So, no tears, OK? I will get home to you tomorrow, even if I have to swim. I will find a way Ellie, but just promise to be good for your nana.'

'I will,' she said in a singsong voice.

'I love you,'

'I wove you,' she said back, and my heart broke more.

My mother came back on the line. 'All sorted. Don't worry now, we'll be fine.'

'You're always to my rescue.'

'You're your mother's daughter. You do the same for your own little one.'

I couldn't answer. If I tried to speak, I would cry.

'Where will you sleep?' She whispered.

'Has to be on the floor of Stansted. It's the only way we can stay in line for a ticket. The desk opens at five in the morning and the battle for a flight starts. Mum, there's only two tickets for the next flight and there are two in front of me.'

'Don't worry about that now. They'll be a way, there always is. You just have to get a good night's sleep and keep the head tomorrow. Half the people going on the next flight might not even show up with the snow.'

'It'll be Christmas Eve mum, everyone who can get to the airport will show up.'

'We'll see. Just concentrate on you. We're going to have a big hot chocolate now with marshmallows and cream and then we are going to read a book all about Santa and then Ellie's going to sleep in the bed with me...' I heard a thumping noise as if Ellie was jumping and smiled at her resilience, '... and we're going to lie in the bed and plan our day tomorrow.'

'Can we go to the park?' Ellie called out.

'Yes, my lovely, we can.' I heard a whoop of joy, then laughter. Even when the world crumbles around them, children still laugh.

'See, Peggy, all will be fine, OK? You just get yourself home, safe.'

'Thanks, mum,' I said. 'I'll text you in the morning once I know something. I'm going to turn my phone off again so I can ring once I know anymore.'

'Do that. We'll be grand. Love you.'

'Love you too,' I said, and hung up.

After hearing the love from the loves of my life, the night without them stretched out longer, the distance between us too far. I longed to be the one standing on the other side of that phone call, holding on to my girl now, telling her and assuring her everything would be alright.

The fight drained from me, and the world darkened. So what if I'd given out food to people? It didn't make me a good person, and it wouldn't get me nearer to Ellie, either. Even speaking to Niall, wasn't it just a repeat of old mistakes? Did I ever learn? I wanted to get on a plane just to be away from myself. I tried to recall another time I'd felt as low. There had been plenty of competition of late, but this was worse. This was much, much worse. Because this time I was all alone. Even though Niall was beside me, who at least was a person I could talk to, or would look after my spot if I needed the bathroom, he was still a complete stranger.

I ran my tongue along my teeth and felt debris and a film on its surface. I was dirty and was sure I smelled too from wearing the same clothes for two days and here I was sitting on a very hard porcelain floor that was trampled all over by thousands of shoes with only a handbag as a pillow and strangers all around me. The lights overhead promised little sleep. It was my turn to stare at the floor.

Rolls

A roll dangled in front of my nose. Niall knelt before me. 'Eat. You looked after everyone in the queue except yourself.'

I took the roll, knowing he was going to keep on at me until I did, but once in my hand, the bile came up in my throat at the thought of eating. I laid it down on the floor.

'Come on, Peggy.'

'A few seconds ago, you didn't even know I'd put food down. What's changed your mood? We're in trouble. It's all pointless. Here we are, destined to spend the night on the floor, and for what? We won't get on that flight tomorrow. Niall, we're stranded.'

Niall sat down beside me and shuffled as close as he could get. He unwrapped my roll first and handed it to me, then done the same with his own and took a bite. He waited until he swallowed to talk.

'Well, see, I have a plan. Eat up, otherwise I won't tell. You're going to need your strength for what I'm suggesting.'

I took the roll. In between bites, he spoke. 'I felt like you earlier.'

'Yeah, I kinda noticed.'

'Again, it was you that shook me out of it. I watched you, Peggy, how your kindness changed the way people, strangers, reacted. One second we were all depressed, now look.'

I looked down the line; it was true I saw more smiles as people ate than earlier. 'So what? Once they're done, they still have a night of pain on this floor. A roll won't cure anybody. And where does it get us? It won't take away any of the problems we're going to face tomorrow.'

'It solved an immediate problem though, didn't it? What you did was so unexpected it changed how they felt. You weren't on the receiving end. You don't know how it felt to be given a loving gesture like you did. And it was Peggy, it was love.' He shook his head. 'When you're low, when you're at your lowest and someone offers even a hint of kindness, it's mood changing... it can be lifesaving.'

'Ah, give over now. Let's get some perspective here. It's only food.'

'To you. Only someone with spare money could do what you did, Peggy. As much as it seems easy, if you only have a couple of brown coins in your pocket, then you run out of options. That roll was more than just food for me because, my dear girl, it's inspired me.'

'How so?'

'Would you say you're short of cash?'

'I wouldn't say I'm on the breadline yet, but I'm getting there.'

He ran his fingers through his hair, thinking, 'OK, I'll rephrase. How much is it worth to you to get home?'

I stopped eating. 'Everything in my bank account.'

'I feel the same. What if we offer these two as much as we can to change places with them? Your gesture, giving them the food, has softened them.'

'Niall, I don't know. I tried that earlier in a toy shop and it didn't go down that well at all. Money can get people's backs up.' I leant in closer. 'You saw the guy next to me having a meltdown earlier. He wants to get home, too.'

'Yeah, well, what if we explain how much we need to get home? You've bought us a way in, at least this way we can try.'

We ate the rest of our roll in silence, and the more I chewed, the more I agreed with Niall. I would do anything it took to get home to my daughter. Five minutes earlier I had seen everyone as the same, all trying to get home, all in it together, all abandoned passengers looking for the end of their journey, searching for a way back to loved ones. Now, as I looked at the two men, I saw them as obstacles, objects that stood in front of me and blocked my way to my daughter. Once past them, I could be on the next flight home. I could walk in the door to my house before Ellie woke up and be there for Christmas Eve. It was time for Game Face Peggy, in a game I didn't know the odds for yet, but would win whatever it cost me. Nothing mattered other than that.

'What do you suggest?' I asked.

Hustle

'Come on, follow my lead,' he said, standing up.

I did as told, and followed him, aware I hung behind like a frightened child, but it was how I felt. This was our only chance, and I didn't want to do anything to mess it up. Niall approached the first man, who was busy finishing his roll. At least he seemed approachable, a man with an amiable face, offering a smile when he saw us. Even though he was my age, about his early forties, the dark circles under his eyes told me he looked as tired as I felt. The second man did not look happy to see us. Niall would need to convince the two of them if it was to work.

'Thanks for the food. How much do I owe you?' The first man asked me.

I waved my hands, making a crisscross gesture. 'No, that's on me. I wanted to give people a treat.'

'It's why I dragged her over here. Her doing that made me think about how there is still some humanity in the world,' Niall said.

'Sometimes, sure, this day has tested that concept though,' the man laughed.

Niall placed his hands together as if in prayer. 'I'm sorry to ask you but if I wasn't desperate, if we weren't desperate, we wouldn't dream of it but we need to get home as soon as we can and we all heard the woman at the desk, there are only two tickets left for the Cork flight. So, we are here to ask you both to name your price.'

The second man in the line screwed up his face. 'Have you a million?'

Niall's laugh came out awkward and desperate. 'Well, no, but...'

'Even if you put down a million right now, I wouldn't sell my ticket. Do I look like I need cash?'

Niall put his hands up in the air, trying to diffuse the situation. 'No, not at all. I'm sorry, I just wanted to explain and hoped money might compensate if we were to buy the ticket slot from you. The last thing I wanted was to offend you.'

'I told you,' I whispered, 'money just gets people's back up.'

The first guy had gone back to eating his roll, while the other guy was staring at me, seething but waiting for one of us to speak.

'Niall didn't mean to upset you. We just want a chance to explain. If I don't ask you, if I don't try everything in my power to get home, I will never forgive myself.'

Angry man sprang from the floor, on his feet in seconds and balling his fists, ready to fight. I recoiled, leaning in to Niall, while hating myself a little for the subservient gesture. Niall puffed out his chest, prepared to duel. The first man touched Angry man's arm, who jerked his body away and for a moment, I thought he might hit him, but then he blew out a long breath, his whole demeanour deflating.

'Why do you think you're the only people desperate to get home? We all have a story, you know? Look around, there's no one in this airport who wants to be here. Why do you think you deserve a ticket more than them?'

'I don't deserve any better, but I need to try anything I can,' Niall said, holding out his hands.

'But you going in front of him means I don't get on that flight. What makes you better than me?'

Before Niall could answer, we heard a man speaking in gruff, threatening tones, coming from further down the line, he was shoving a guy three people down, and once he had pushed the man, he lost his own balance and let go of his grip. Stumbling, he ended up on the floor and lolling his head from side to side, his view settled over to the desk beside us. I could almost see the light bulb ping on above his head. Wobbling on getting up, he walked, staggered more like, in our direction.

'What's happening, lads?' he slurred. He stopped in the gap of the queue Niall and I had left and despite his drunkenness, he made a formidable presence. He was well over six foot, and could pass for a rugby player. His chest was the size of two well-built men and his wide-legged, arms resting on his hips stance, although unbalanced, was full of menace. This guy wanted trouble.

'You all right there?' Second man, angry man, now somehow my angry man compared to this other angry man asked, matching the rugby fellas threatening behaviour even though the other was twice the size.

'I am, yeah. Just getting in line.'

'Well, the line starts at the back of the queue. Go join it.'

Angry guy was growing on me.

'Make me.' the man roared at the top of his voice. It had the same result as if he had just shot a gun, a booming, burst your eardrums sort of noise.

There were no staff around. No security or airline people. Nobody left to step in and sort it out. We were on our own.

Niall stood alongside Angry man. 'Go on now.'

'Fuck you,' the man said, leaning forward, stumbling again, so he put his hand out to stop himself and ended up squatting. He turned it around though, turning his fall into a sitting position.

'This looks like a grand spot for me,' he said, taking a slug from his beer.

'Get up. Now,' Angry man said.

'Make me,' Rugby fella said, snarling, then finding it hilarious, laughing at the top of his voice. The night just got very long. Happy with an audience, he drank the can in long gulps and finished it. He then reached into his pocket and fished out another. Popping the top, he slugged that back, too.

The people behind him recoiled, moving back to give him more space. It was a good idea because the man was unstable. His eyes and movements were unsteady, his body swayed and threatened to tip forward than back. The only sound out of him was the repeated belches. One eye was closed at that stage. None of us moved. As the guy drank, we watched him transfixed, like a nature show where you know something bad is about to happen, but dare not move in case the animal pounced.

As he finished the second can, it proved too much for even a big man like him, and his head lulled, his chin bobbing until it rested on his chest. Less than a minute later, his other eye gave up the fight and closed. The empty can stayed upright in his hand.

'Help me move him,' Angry man said to Niall.

Niall shifted position to walk around. First man shook his head. 'Leave him awhile.'

'Why?' Angry guy asked. 'He shouldn't get to skip the queue.'

Rugby fella roared, 'I'll fight the lot of ye.'

'See?' The first man in the queue said. 'Just wait. The drink is too close to him yet. Fight him when the hangover comes.'

Drool dribbled out of the side of Rugby fella's mouth, and a combination of noises escaped: a cross between a snore and a hiccup and a heave.

'There he blows,' First man said.

Rugby fella projectile vomited a tidal wave of sick in front of him, landing in a straight line across the cream floor. It kept on coming, becoming less of a wave and more like a spray, and ended in a splatter. Once finished, he didn't even seem to notice the destruction he had just caused to the sleeping arrangements, just turned and lay on his side. At the exact spot Niall and I had sat. I dashed over and scooped up both our bags so they didn't get hit with further vomit. Drunk man, oblivious, without scooping at his mouth or making sure he wasn't lying in his own sick, fell asleep.

'What the actual?' Angry man said, going to pick the guy up.

'Leave him,' First man said. 'Let him sleep it off. He's safe on his side. The airport staff can deal with him when they get in.'

'We've nowhere to lie down now, though,' Niall said.

'I've a suggestion. You said you wanted a chance to explain. It sounds to me we all have a reason to want to get home. How about since I'm the first in line, I let you state your case? We each tell our story. At the end we each cast a vote.'

'That's stupid. We'll all choose our own,' Angry man said.

'We won't be able to choose our own.'

'Sure, then these two will just choose each other.'

First man shrugged. 'Well then, me and you get the casting vote. It's going to be a long night. We may as well have something to do in the meantime. We'll budge up so you can sleep alongside us. If you can't convince us, we will at least back you up in the morning about what happened with old hollow legs here and explain why you're both out of the line. What do you think?'

For the first time in hours, I felt like smiling. I hugged Niall because he had given me this, an opportunity, a way in to convince them. From now on, it was up to me.

'I'm in.' I grinned.

'Me too,' Niall said.

We both stood opposite the two men. Once First man sat, we sat too, leaving Angry man standing. He crossed his arms and huffed for a moment, but then, making his contempt known, sat opposite Niall and me, forming a circle, us against them.

First man rummaged in his bag and pulled out a bottle of brandy. 'Right so, let's get some loose lips on ye. I don't know about you, but I could do with a drink.' He rummaged some more and pulled out a four pack of expensive looking brandy glasses. He shrugged at my raised eyebrow. ‘Who would’ve thought you’d buy Irish crystal in an English airport, eh? Meant to be a Christmas present, but my father-in-law will understand.’ He tore the packaging open and laid the glasses in a line on the floor. Then he unscrewed the bottle and poured an equal measure into each glass. The smell of brandy, sharp and fiery, wafted over, replacing the vomit that had invaded my nostrils. ‘I’m Donal. Now, who’s going to start us off?’

Sing For Your Supper

I cradled the brandy in both hands and took a sip. The liquid burned my throat as it went down, giving me a warm feeling that spread out from my lips to my cheeks, flushing them. My chest felt it too, a comforting cloak from my heart to my shoulders. It would give courage, just not enough yet.

'Come on then, let's all hear this story that's going to keep me here,' Angry man said. He hadn't touched his brandy.

Niall sat up straighter. 'I can go first if that's all right with you, Peggy?'

'Please do,' I said.

'I'm Niall, and this is Peggy. We now know Donal. If I'm going to tell you a story, can I get your name?'

Angry man stared at his brandy, swirling the liquid around the glass. 'Aidan,' he said, not looking up.

'OK then, Aidan. Here goes,' he looked at the ceiling and muttered, 'where to start, where to start.'

I thought I knew the story that was going to come out of Niall, about his kids and sharing Christmas but I was wrong.

'My story starts when I was a little boy and living in Cork.'

Aidan groaned. 'So we're going to get your whole life story?'

'It's just a little back story, but it's significant to what I have to say.'

'One story is all everyone's getting. Let him tell it whatever way he wants,' Donal said.

'Thank you,' Niall said. 'Sorry Aidan, now that I think about it, my story starts even earlier, before I even arrived. I was an only child born to Doris Reid, an unwed mother who had to fight in Catholic Ireland in the late seventies to keep me. In other houses, she would have had to go to one of those places, one of those that we hear so much about these days. My mother was one of the lucky ones. Her parents cared more about loving her than what people thought and were only on the surface religious. They kept her at home, so she went unnoticed. They put no pressure on her to give me up, only demanding her secrecy and insisting she hide in the house so she could have options when the baby came, so she could adopt me out to a family if she wanted. My mother had left the little village in West Cork years before, so she went unnoticed. When the time came to handing me over, she refused, so her family bought a gold band to wear and concocted a tale of her needing to flee her abusive husband in England. Many of the women would understand a married woman fleeing rather than the overused lie of a dead one. If it had been ten or twenty years earlier, it would have been a different story, and the village would have shunned her. Maybe because of that, or more to do with my grandparents' outward bravado, they accepted Doris back into the fold. I lived a life of fields and freedom, of poverty and getting by, of hunger and wishes, long hours reading and daydreaming. A country boy with nothing to do but dream and in those fields, I often lay on my back and imagined going to the city and making my fortune.'

Aidan sighed. 'Get to the point. By this stage, we'll be still listening to his story when the desk opens.'

'We're stuck here, aren't we? With nowhere else to go. What's your rush? It passes the time which is fine by me. You'll be able to talk as much as you want when it's your turn.' Donal said.

'Ah, but you see, Aidan, it's important you know this about me as it's instrumental to my reason to get home. Can I go on? Or are you going to interrupt me every two seconds?'

Aidan made a zip pulling across the lips gesture, and Niall carried on.

'My mother never spoke about my father. For years I didn't even know his name, never asked for it, never had a need as she gave me enough love for the two of them and I had my uncle Joe, my mother's brother and my grandfather to show me the ways and differences of men. But there is a time in a person's life when they question who they are and where they came from and I was no different. For me, it was a family tree project in school. There was a whole other side to my life that was blank. Where did I get my dark hair from? All my family were brown-haired, light brown more so whereas my hair was almost black and my eyes were different too. One day, I asked her straight out. 'What was my father's name?' and my mother burst out crying. She went to her bed and cried for two days non-stop. By the end of her tears, her skin was thinner and burnt bright red under her bloodshot eyes and her nose was raw from the amount of snot that had passed through her and, along with it, the desire to know had left me. Her voice was hoarse when she called out to me to come over. By the time she was ready to talk, I wasn't ready to hear because if that question could do that to her, I didn't want to know the answer.'

Niall looked up at the ceiling and caught his breath. 'That question has haunted me my whole life. I never brought it up again, and my mother never mentioned it. It changed something between us. It created an uneasiness, a distrust, between me and her. It was the son of the sergeant, Michael Dooley, a boy I hated, a nasty pig who loved to terrorise the lads in the village and got away with it because of who his dad was, it was him who told me who my father was. One day as I had him against the wall for beating up a young fella in the school. I still remember his face as he said it, how he relished the changing look on mine as he revealed the one thing that was my weakness. My mother took the blame for that, for giving him a way to get to me, but also for telling someone other than me about my father. I called Martin Dooley a liar and gave him a black eye as punishment, a gesture that had his own father knocking at our door and giving me a whipping that left me unable to sit for a week. Even though she begged, I never told her the reason I fought him. Before that, they had known me for sorting people out if they started. A finisher, not a starter. Mad but fair, so she knew, knew he had provoked me, but I said nothing, showing her I could keep secrets too and whether it was that, or if it was the cold way I changed towards her, she said nothing. After, I couldn't wait to get away. For the rest of my years, I kept my head down in school and studied hard enough to buy myself the only way out of there, a scholarship to UCC, to Cork City. And I never went back, not never, that's not right. The visits for birthdays or near Christmas were made, but I never stayed again, only ever staying an hour, two at the most. I wouldn't mean to act like that. Each drive down I swore to myself it would be the time we'd talk, clear the air, find a way. I'd even wrote scripts. As soon as I'd walk in the door and see her, I'd want to turn around and leave. The love on her face, the way she lit up when she saw me, killed me, because it was a face full of secrets and she wouldn't share them with me. It killed me because I loved seeing her light up. Yet I couldn't find a way past it. So, I kept it up, kept the pretence going, never mentioning my father's name. I should have told her what Michael said because from that day on it was different between us, with her stilted, straightening up whenever I was around, waiting, waiting for either a fight or an accusation that never came. Me the opposite, I folded in whenever I was around her, I hunched down, with nothing to say because what could I say? She was still the woman who gave me life, who gave me a start when others couldn't, who helped me and fought for me even when I was in the womb, even before she knew me. The woman who I have heard now is dying, who I might not even get to see in time. She has asked for me, got my Uncle Joe to call and say she desperately wants to talk, to tell me what I need to hear, who is finally ready to talk and it's all so sad because I'm finally going to hear the story of what made me yet I'm terrified because to hear it means I'm losing my mother, to hear it means she's ready to go. That's not what I wanted. What I wanted was to know what happened and then mend us, not say goodbye, I'm not ready to say goodbye.'

Niall buried his head in his hands. Donal took Niall's empty glass and topped it up. 'You've earned another.'

Niall took his wet hands away and nodded at Donal. 'Thanks,' he said and picked up the glass, cradling it in two hands as if it omitted heat. He sniffed its contents.

'She's not old. She was only eighteen when she fell pregnant with me, only turned sixty this year. I thought she had more time. Thought I had more time to fix us. Once I had my own children, I understood more but didn't too, if that makes sense? I understood her love, or the need to shield a child from pain, the way you would fight for them, kill for them, what I didn't get, what I couldn't understand was the coldness about explaining about my father, or why she would still keep from me what she knew I needed. After Michael told me his name, I did something I knew was wrong. I waited for the Saturday when my mother went food shopping, something I helped with, but seeing as I couldn't walk properly after the sergeant booted me around the place, I could get away with it. As soon as she left, I sneaked into her room and searched every inch of that place, trying to find something, anything, that told me about him. In an old suitcase that I had to jimmy the lock, I found a yellowed newspaper clipping, a piece touched so many times, by a finger ran along the words of it over and over, it smudged and disintegrated. There on the first line was the same name Michael Dooley had spat at me. I could make out it was from Kent, but the date was illegible. All I could make out was the title, Hero saves woman. I've lived in England for years now and I know I could go to Kent and dig around, find the man or news on the man, but that was never what I wanted. What I wanted was for her to tell me. To want me enough to tell me. That's what drove me mad all these years. She didn't love me enough to give me the one thing she knew I wanted.'

Niall took a sip of brandy, then stared at the floor. 'That's it. I'm done. That's the reason I need to get home. They say she might have another day, or it might only be hours but one thing is for sure, a week from now I won't have a mother and if I don't get there in time, I will never find out what she wants to tell me about my father either. Worse than that, even, I might never talk to her again, I won't ever be able to make things right between us.'

'I'm so sorry,' I said to Niall. He looked at me as if he had only just realised there were other people in his company, and I saw the reason for his haunted look. He was already mourning her.

'I'm sorry, too,' Aidan said. 'Are you finished?'

Niall nodded.

'All right, Peggy, you're up.'

'Whoa there, horsie,' Donal said, laughing.

'Well, there's no point messing around. I need to know what's so important they need to take my plane ticket. Come on Peggy, spill it.'

And so I did.

Spill

'I feel embarrassed following Niall now but I'm going to plead my case just the same because, for me, or rather my daughter, it is life and death. That's who I want to get back to. I just want to get home to Ellie. When I left her the other day, she didn't want me to leave, like intuition or something, she said there would be a problem and I wouldn't get home, that I'd miss Christmas. I laughed at that and shrugged it off but seeing the fear in her, I made her a promise that no matter what, I would be there when she woke up on Christmas morning and now, I don't know if I can. Coming here was a mistake. It's karma, I think. Putting a man first instead of doing the motherly thing and staying at home with my child.' I hung my head, not wanting to see their judgment. 'It's the reason I'm stuck here. It's mortifying to admit this, to tell strangers my mistakes, but I will do anything it takes to get you to understand why I have to get on that flight. Here goes.' I shouldn't have looked at them; they all watched me. Niall gave an encouraging nod. I closed my eyes for the next bit.

'My story starts with me sneaking out of a hotel room this morning. You can imagine how that goes. All the clichés were there, the sleeping man in the bed, the struggling to get dressed in the dark and, more so, doing it in silence so I wouldn't wake him up. All the usual shame you'd expect as I walked along the corridor. Knowing I didn't even brush my hair or teeth because I was in such a rush to see him, I hopped on a plane without even packing. I popped into the hotel bathroom and couldn't bear to look at myself. I never imagined I would be the kind to have an affair. That person wasn't me. I felt such shame as I looked at my reflection. For the things I'd did in that hotel room. For leaving my daughter. For the recklessness of jumping on a plane. None of that was ever me.'

I picked at a loose thread in my trousers.

'There is an excuse for my madness. Two months ago, I found a note on my bedside locker from my husband. It was just one sentence, just words on a piece of paper, but those five words destroyed my life. *I can't do it anymore.* Beside the note was his phone and house keys. Isn't that so final? Who would leave behind their phone these days? My first instinct was that he was out somewhere trying to top himself. I ran down to the woods behind our garden in my nightdress and checked every tree, not thinking about what I would do if I found him hanging from one. It was like blind, frantic, distracted, confusion. I was wild and desperate. After the woods were clear, I followed the path to the little strip of beach and checked along the sand for his shoes. There was nothing. Then reason came to me again, and I remembered I was holding my phone in my hand. I rang the guards, and they told me to first ring around his friends and then check our money and his wardrobe. I was in the middle of trying to arrange a search party when I checked our joint bank account. He'd paid for a flight a month beforehand and while I was out searching Knockfarraig Woods, he was eating brunch in a Michelin starred restaurant in London. Leaving his phone at home meant there was no way to ring him. He'd blocked me on social media. I sent email after email with no reply. I even contacted his work, which was embarrassing when they explained he had handed his notice in two months before. Two months. All that time, he planned and plotted. Once I found that out, I stopped acting desperate. There was no point, and I had to give up the ghost that was ghosting me. Fast forward to this week when I saw my four-year-old daughter's Christmas wish list. In the corner at the very top of the page was a drawing of a man and a woman holding hands with a little girl in the middle by the Christmas tree. I asked her what she wanted me to write on her list and she answered: Daddy. That broke me. I had to try one last time for her. I emailed him asking would he meet me and was shocked when he replied. Without thinking, I was on the next available flight. My mother thought I was crazy, but agreed I had to go. I thought I could convince him. I tried. Seeing him brought so many emotions up. I forgot I should be angry with him for leaving us, for not even checking how we were or how we were surviving, but I was just so relieved, you know?'

The others nodded.

'I was so happy to see him alive and real and next to me, I fell into him, into the way we were, the way we had always handled our arguments, falling in to bed and talking after. Afterwards, the questions I should have asked first, the truth, came out. He told me all about his new life, and the new woman he'd left me for, the woman he had no intention of leaving now. I lay there in the dark and felt stupid for thinking we would have a chance. On the phone, he had acted like he wanted me again, encouraged me to come, and I was foolish enough to feel excitement for the first time in years. Years. John didn't do the right thing by us, or by Ellie, and why would he? After fifteen years, you would think I would have learned that. Even if he wanted to explain in person the reasons he left, I would have understood, but to make out there was still a chance, to treat me like we were getting back together was too much. When I asked him how he could sleep with me if he loved her, do you know what he said?'

The others didn't answer, just shook their heads.

'He said, "I loved you first." For him, it was that simple, like as if sleeping with me didn't even count, that being with me before allowed him to go there again. As the hours went by, I lay in the dark and wondered how he could put his feelings in compartments like that, and I tried to see it from his point of view. For him, it was the best way to say goodbye. I wanted to say, "Your vows meant you should have loved me last, too." But what good would it have done? He decided. He loved her now. Can you have an affair with your husband? When he's with someone else, to me, it is cheating. How sad was I to think I could fix things? All I did was prove I'm a failure and put my whole daughter's Christmas in jeopardy. I snuck out of that room before he woke because if I didn't, if I'd waited for him to wake, I would have begged him to come home. Doing that would mean seeing he didn't want to, that he didn't love me anymore and I wasn't ready for that. Even after all that, I'm still not ready.'

I laughed.

'He didn't even bring Miss Rainbow.'

'Miss Rainbow?' Aidan cut in.

'Yeah, it's this rainbow coloured doll that will be the death of me. Before I flew, I explained how impossible it was to get that toy in Ireland, sold out everywhere and Ellie wanted it desperately, and he assured me he would get it in London. When I asked him, he acted like he didn't even remember. Just pointed to a bag full of crap from the hotel shop. How can I go back to her without her dad and the toy she wanted? I am such a fool. Sleeping with him meant something to me. It was the new start we needed. But I saw a start, when he saw a goodbye. After I slept with him, after I learned the truth, I watched him sleep without a care in the world, knowing he had broken my heart again, knowing he would break our daughter's heart and I wondered how I could still love him.'

My voice caught and the rest of the words came out croaky. I gasped for air through it, having to get the words out, it hurt to say them out loud.

'He wasn't a good person. Yet I'd have gone back in a second. So, now you know. I'm a failure and a fool. But one thing I've never been is too proud. That's why I'm here now, sitting in front of you three, asking you to choose me to be the one who gets sent home. I couldn't give Ellie her daddy for Christmas or the only toy she wanted, either. One of her parents has to be there.'

'Thanks, Peggy,' Donal said.

Niall smiled, his lips uneasy on his face. I wasn't sure if Niall forced his smile for my benefit, or if it was just from how he was feeling or from pity, or because I was someone other than he thought I was.

I took a sip of brandy, more so I wouldn't have to look at any of them.

Aidan huffed.

'What?' I asked.

'Nothing,' he said.

'It's not nothing. You're angry.'

'That's not love,' he said.

'What would you know about love?' I spat. 'Love is giving something of yourself to someone, even if it means you have to suffer to give it. Love is following a man anywhere, if it means your daughter smiles. It's a strand of hair draped across the child's face for comfort when she needs to feel you are near. It's a cancelled night out you've looked forward to for months when a fever appears. Or holding back their hair when the stomach bug attacks in the middle of the night and you have to rub their back or their tummy as they cry in pain, when all you want to do is take it from them, take their suffering yourself, so exhausted you could cry, the smell strong enough to make you vomit too. And after you clean all the shit and vomit up because that is it, that is love. It's giving every part of yourself over to another in order to help them. But you probably have never done that in your life. It's so normal for you to flip out to get what you want, and it works. You're so selfish you think everyone else is that way too.'

He shook his head slowly, his eyes wounded. 'I meant him. What he did to you wasn't love,' Aidan said.

My already flushed cheeks burned.

Aidan got to his feet. 'I need a walk.' None of us spoke as he marched the full length of the line of lying down or sitting people and, passing them, continued on.

'If he went any faster, there would be sparks coming off him,' Niall said.

Donal nudged me. 'You all right?'

I nodded, embarrassed. Niall stayed watching Aidan, who disappeared around the corner at the end of the terminal. I stood before he looked back at me, needing to get away from the awkward situation. 'May as well use the chance to go to the bathroom.'

This time, the bathroom had no one standing outside. Nobody cared anymore about leaving their bag. There was nowhere to go and everyone stuck here had worse worries than that.

Red patched spattered over my cheeks, and my hair hung over my shoulders in unbrushed strags. A red rim surrounded my eyelids and dulled the blue colour of my eyes. The dark circles under them looked like deep hollows of scooped out skin. The bloodshot lines in my sclera pointed like arrows to my iris. I looked a mess.

Telling my story had shone a light on my failures and left me exposed and empty. I had told the truth, and now it was time to admit it to myself. All these months I had kept it together for Ellie, for my mother, only crying at night when I turned off the lights and lay alone. I missed my husband. I missed the way my heart quickened when I heard his keys turn in the door. Or the way he made me feel when he smiled at me. When he touched me. The man who had been my best friend, who had been my lover and the father of my child, didn't love me anymore, and I had to accept it. It had felt good to sleep with him. Not just to get back together. Not just for Ellie's sake, but for me as a woman. It had felt good to feel wanted again.

I patted my cheeks with water, needing to calm the flush from the brandy down. Hot to the touch, the cold water was welcome on my skin. Wasn't there more to what I was feeling? It bothered me that my story might bother Niall. How could that be when I still wanted my husband? The worse thing I could do was start up something with another man when I wasn't ready. Yet I already felt I needed Niall. His opinion already mattered.

I brushed my hair with my fingers, and once my skin settled to pink salmon instead of red lobster, I braved the line again. The walk through the check-in desks was eerie, with the lights off. With no flights going, people queued at their designated desks rather than down those aisles, and I quickened my pace. Two men watched me return.

'Where's Aidan?' I asked.

'Out for a smoke. Should be back any minute,' Donal said.

'Here he is,' Niall said. 'Feeling better?'

'Too long without nicotine,' Aidan said, giving a smile.

'I'm sorry,' I said. 'I took out what I was feeling on you.'

He nodded. 'Forgotten,' he said.

'You're up if you want to go next,' Niall said.

We all settled into the places we had claimed before. I sat with my legs crossed and waited.

Aidan tapped the floor. 'My story is different. Peggy is right. In the how sad is my story or how innocent am I plea, I'm going to lose. It was still mine though,' he said those last words to me.

He lifted his untouched brandy glass and drained it. 'I've listened to two of you now, and there's no comparison. Against a story about a dying mother or a little girl needing her mum, I'm never going to win. And I'll tell you, I don't deserve the ticket, so let Donal go on and tell you his and ye can fight it out among the three of you. I'm taking myself out of the game.'

'No, it doesn't work like that,' Niall said. 'The four of us get to decide who we vote for. You are in that spot, fair and square. It's our job to convince you.'

'That's what I'm saying. I'm convinced. Job done. Get on the plane and see ya later. All you have to do now is convince Donal. I'm out.'

'I'd still like to hear why you'd like to get home. I shouldn't have judged you. Anyway, hearing someone else's misery makes me feel better about myself,' I said.

My stab at humour worked. Aidan gave me a questioning look, and when he saw my smirk, he smiled, then shook his head, and his face fell again.

'I'm not like all of you. In my story, I'm the bad guy.'

'Hello? Did you not hear mine? I left my daughter Christmas week to sleep with a man who abandoned us. I can promise you there will be no judgment on my part at least.'

'Nor on mine,' Niall said.

'I'm just glad to be sitting here churning the time. Anyway, if your story makes you look bad, it's only going to make mine look even better, so help me out,' Donal said.

Aidan took a deep breath. 'Where do I start? Do I start at the beginning like Niall or the end like Peggy? I could do both. I don't have a redeeming story of love from a parent. My mother left me when I was ten and the only problem I had with her going was that she didn't take me with her. My father was nasty, man,' he rubbed at his jaw, running his fingers along the day old stubble. 'He was the kind of guy if you saw the belt in his hands you were relieved because at least it wasn't the baseball bat. I spent my entire childhood avoiding him or hiding. I ran away loads of times but living outside is tough and they always found me and sent me back or I gave myself up. In the summer months I could brave it out, either walking around till it got dark and hiding in a bush somewhere, but when the winter came, with nothing to sleep on in the rain and nothing to keep you warm when the temperatures dropped, I figured whatever he did to me was better than pneumonia. Care wasn't an option either, I couldn't handle that.'

He stopped as Donal topped up his brandy. Lifting the glass, he tilted it at Donal and took a small sip.

'Cheers, man. The last time I returned, I worked out I had to leave the smart way, a permanent way, bit like you Niall, but I'd lost out on too much school to catch up and get the results, so at seventeen, I found another way to leave, ran more like, to a different county for an apprenticeship. There, nobody knew who my blood was. I could be someone new, but it still rubs off, doesn't it? Life tested me, I won't lie. And I blew with an anger I never knew could be inside me, the same anger I ran from and for years, I hated myself. Pushing people away, being a dick and knowing it. Once I made some money, I did a bit of counselling, but the demons were a bit too rough coming out, so I quit. The main thing I took away from those sessions was I had a choice. I could choose how my life turned out. And then I met Nancy.'

His face erupted in the first proper smile I'd seen from him.

'She had lived in my town and growing up I had always liked her but thought she was way above my league. I had been going with another girl back then, anyway. And then one day she was there in the town I lived in. It felt like fate or something. I saw her walk along the street and I just thought wow, if I had a girl like her next to me, I would be the happiest man alive and then she looked right at me and smiled and I felt an opening inside me I can't describe, even now I can't remember approaching her, it was like my body took over, somebody else said the right words to convince her to give me a chance and go out with me and she was everything special I'd heard I should feel but never had. It was like switching electricity on. Nancy made me feel good, made me want to do good. There followed the best few years of my life.'

Aidan stopped to take a drink, his smile turning downwards.

'But of course, I fucked it up. That poor girl. Even in the early days of dating, I didn't even know what I was doing half the time, let alone her figuring out. I would give her a little, then pull back. I would make promises to meet then not show, with her thinking I had forgot or chosen to do something else when, I was hugging myself in my room, rocking myself to sleep, convinced that I was doing her a favour, that she deserved better than me because being in love brought out the best side in me but it also brought out something I didn't want, another side that I despised.'

He drained his glass.

'Like if we were laughing about something, and we stopped to look at each other, two thoughts would run through my mind. The first would be I had never looked at such a beautiful girl up close, her eyes like nothing I'd ever seen before, and the urge to kiss her came from deep inside my whole body. As she looked back at me with pure love, I would feel an urge to dig my nails into her cheeks and stretch her face and tell her she was the stupidest bitch I'd ever met.'

Aidan met my open-mouthed stare.

'It's hard not to judge that, isn't it?'

He straightened up.

'I never acted on it, but I had those compulsions all the time. If she asked me an innocent question, or made a funny remark, my first reaction was to throw something or smash something and the anger would flick on like a kettle, the bubbling getting more and more until I would have to get out of the room or the place, and get away from her so she wouldn't see, so she wouldn't notice. Sometimes it leaked out. She wasn't dumb, but I never blew with her, never around her. I'd run away and start on a stranger if they pushed up against me or I'd go for a run and scream on this hill near us or out to the dump and smash something up. At night I'd lie in bed next to her and worry myself stupid about what if I actually lost it with her? I didn't understand why loving her could make me so angry. The best way I could handle it was to push her away. It tied me in knots, holding it in, wound me so tight because the only way to cope was to hold everything in until it got too much and I would have to escape out of there. And in the end, even though I never lost it, it still was too much for her. She still decided she didn't want me.'

He closed his eyes.

'By that stage, we lived in England. As an electrician I could get work anywhere, so when her job offered her more money to get a project up and running for five years in London, I encouraged her. On our own, with no friends, we did well, better than I thought we would. The problem was, she wanted kids. Even on our first date, she talked about having children, and I could feel the clock ticking down once the five years were ending. Her plan, our plan, was once the job finished, we would move back to Ireland, hopefully with a bump, all nice and sown up. The more she went on about it, the more I felt those urges, and the more I knew I couldn't go there. If my wife could cause that type of reaction inside of me when she was doing nothing wrong, there would be no stopping me with my children. My father's compulsions were inside of me, too. Instead of speaking to her about it, I took the coward's way and picked and belittled and pushed her. In fairness, she lasted a lot longer than I would have thought, eventually though, she had enough, and confirmed what I had known from the day I met her. That she was too good for me. After the five years, she moved back to Ireland, and I stayed here and I told myself it was for the best. Until this morning, when I bumped into a friend from Cork. He mentioned she's with another guy and right then my heart broke and like that day I saw her, without thinking, I ran to my car and booked to get on the next flight and now it's delayed and I've been talking myself out of it because she's happier without me, and who am I to show up at her door at Christmas and tell her how much I still love her? Who am I to want to tell her the reasons I'm so screwed up?'

Aidan's mouth puckered and even though his face made the actions to speak, opening and closing, no words came out. I shuffled up to him and placed a hand on his back, not wanting to startle him, but he turned to me and embraced me and I held him as he fought to find his breath.

'I'm sorry,' he said.

'Don't be.'

'For what my opinion is worth, I think you should go,' Niall said. 'I often wonder how different my life might have been if I'd fought for my wife, if I'd made any gesture to show her the spark could still be there. I should have fought. At the very least, your wife deserves to know the truth. Even if it's just to move on for both of you.'

'That's what Carol thinks too.' Aidan reddened, then ran his finger along the rim of the glass. 'I went to a different therapist. After we split up, even though I got what I thought I wanted, I sank. The only option I could see was killing myself. I figured if I could do that, the least I could do was work out if there was anything else I could do first. Looks like I've worked through my demons too late.'

'It might not be too late.'

'But what if it is? Turning up on Christmas Eve is a bit tragic, isn't it?'

'Or dead romantic, depending how you look at it.'

'That's it though, I don't know how she'll take it.'

'Only one way to find out. I think you should take a chance. Love is worth it,' I said. It got me thinking and a need to smoke came over me so strong I couldn't help myself.

'Guys, can we pause the storytelling for a moment? I think the brandy has gone to my head a little. I need some fresh air.'

'I need the bathroom, anyway. At least this time I'm all right to leave my suitcase.' Aidan said, smiling.

Taking my bag, I made the short walk to outside the terminal and breathed in fresh air for the first time in fifteen hours. All I could think about was John. Aidan had unearthed something, rummaged around the surface of my life and as he spoke, I'd felt like it was digging up buried memories I still couldn't remember and it was bothering me.

Even though John had been the one to do wrong by me, it was me that had acted like I was the one that needed to be sorry. Whether from the brandy or the conversation, I needed answers. I fished in my bag and found my phone and pressed the power button about a hundred times before it kicked into gear, having to do it before I changed my mind. I typed fast and pressed send before I could reason myself out of it.

Why don't you love me anymore? Did I turn you off?

The phone beeped while my thumbs still hovered mid air: *You did nothing wrong.*

The phone beeped again, and I wondered how John could think that quick, let alone text. *You're a brilliant mother to Ellie.*

What did that mean? I watched the dots that told me he was typing.

But when you became a mum, I lost a wife. You used to be so into me. I could ask anything of you and you'd do it, like I was your everything. When the baby came, you changed. You had another interest - and it wasn't me. I couldn't handle the lack of attention.

He was talking about four years ago.

Have you been cheating on me for four years?

It's not your doing, it's mine. I looked elsewhere instead of sorting it. I'm sorry.

Before I'd even finished reading, the phone beeped again.

Being with you last night reminded me of what we used to be like before Ellie. We could be like that again.

I hated my heart for skipping a beat, for my first thoughts going to there still being a chance. Before another text could come through or I could say anymore or lead it somewhere I wasn't sure I wanted to go, I turned off the phone again. There was still another story to listen to yet.

In my bag, I found what I was looking for and fished out the old, battered pack of cigarettes I had taken to carrying around with me since John left. Like a comfort blanket, they were my reassurance that if things got bad, I could spark one up. Now was the time. Just as I popped a wonky one in my mouth, Niall appeared at my side.

'Busted,' I said.

'I was hoping you might have some.'

'I haven't smoked in years. They have to be stale, but I don't care. Today warrants one.'

'Oh, I agree. I'll be bold too if you've got one to share.'

'Ha, we can both fall together,' I said, handing him over a bent cigarette. 'Only thing is I've no lighter. I reasoned if I got the urge to want one, the time it would take to get a lighter might talk me out of it. It's worked each time so far.'

'We can't smoke here, anyway.' He pointed to a cluster of ten people standing at the side. 'We have to go to the smoking area. Plenty there we can bum a light from.'

The snow was melting and because of the cold and the constant walkers over the pavement; it had compacted and froze to ice. It was dangerous and slippy. For the second time that day, I cursed wearing my dressy boots, useless in this weather, which now slid out from under me and I went to fall down, only for Niall, who caught hold of my shoulder and stopped me from hitting the floor. The warmth of him, the strength of him, was welcome. He helped me to standing, pulling me closer, his grip holding me steady against the ice that threatened to make me horizontal. 'I won't make it if you let go,' I said.

'I'm not letting go,' he said, his breath dividing into two halves on my face. 'Keep hold of my hand.'

He guided me to the smoking area and I couldn't help but notice how good it felt to have a hand guide me again, to feel a warm palm holding mine. My desperation for love disgusted me. Niall deposited me in a corner of the cordoned off section of the smoking line. Being covered, it was at least shielded from the cold and the ground was dry and clear, relaxing me a little. Niall approached the nearest person and came back, waving the bummed light. His cheeks were as flushed as mine from the brandy. I couldn't decide if it was a chill or a thrill that ran through me as he came close. All I knew was it differed from the way I saw John, whose memory I mixed up in love and pain. With Niall there was a sense of serendipity, a sense we were meant to meet, that being here together was momentous, life changing even, that between the four of us, our conversations were leading us to the answers we had sought, in some of our cases, all our life, or, at least for me, since my marriage existed. With Niall, I sensed kindred spirits: we had shared our pain tonight, both admitting we were dealing with demons we could help each other through. A closeness crept between us.

'You sure you want to do this?' he said.

'Damn right. I'm allowed in these circumstances. Anyway, I'm not myself. These last few days, I've reverted to a teenager and did things I wouldn't have dreamed of doing. I've felt things I haven't allowed myself to feel in years. After these last couple of months, I deserve some fun.'

'Me too,' he said, and lit him and me up. I giggled after the nicotine hit the back of my throat and made me splutter. And then I closed my eyes and just enjoyed it.

'I think you're wrong,' Niall said.

'For what?'

'You said you put a man first before staying at home with Ellie at Christmas time, but I think that was kind of selfless of you. You put aside the things he did. Abandoning you without explanation, the affair, the upping sticks and leaving you to worry about how you would survive. You pushed all that away to salvage a relationship for the sake of your daughter. That's pretty heroic, if you ask me.'

'You think so? Or is that another way of saying I was pretty stupid?'

'Depends on what you think you should do now.'

I took a puff. 'Hmm. I've never been a quitter.'

'It's not quitting if it's the other person throwing in the towel.'

I blew out a long line of smoke and cocked my head to look at him.

'Sorry about your mother. I hope you get home in time.'

'Me too,' he said.

'Did you ever think there might be a reason she never told you?'

'What do you mean?' He screwed up his eyes as he took another drag.

'I don't know, but it seems to me she protected you your whole life. Maybe she was protecting you from that, too?'

The red in Niall's cheeks drained, and with the moonlight hitting his face, a yellow glow fell on him, making him even paler.

'God, I'm sorry, I know nothing. It's just a mother trying to think like another mother, that's all. I'm sorry.'

He stamped his feet and hugged himself to stop the cold. When he spoke, his breath came out pure white in the black sky. 'The problem is, Peggy, I think you're right. I think I've always known that, but I wouldn't admit it. To do so means something horrible caused her pregnancy, something unspeakable. I didn't want to accept that my existence might have brought pain to my mother.'

'It doesn't matter to a mum what pain she goes through to get her baby. It all falls away when they hand them to you.'

'You think so?'

'I do. She proved it to you, didn't she? You said she was brilliant growing up. Seems to me she loved you very much. Seems to me there won't be any grudges either on her part.'

Niall placed a hand on either side of my arms, standing close enough to lean in for a hug or a kiss, and I didn't flinch. A little thrill ran up my arms from the contact, from the possibility of more contact. 'Thank you,' he said, and let go.

I hated myself for wanting a grieving man to kiss me when I had only left another man's bed that very morning, a man that was, still on legal paper anyway, my husband. A man I had messaged only ten minutes beforehand.

'What about you?'

'What about me?'

'Seems your time and needs didn't come into play at all.'

I stiffened, folded my arms. 'Being happy was all I needed.'

'In a family, children aren't a one-parent job, a mum doesn't have to do it all.'

'Do you believe that's true?'

'I do,' he said, looking me straight in the eye.

'See, I always hear all this talk of equal rights and shared parenting, but I rarely see it. It's nice to say how it should be but, well, in reality the roles are as divided now as the sixties.'

'How so?' Niall said, questioning me.

'OK, tell me this: how many nappies did you change in your marriage?'

'Honest answer? At least one a day.'

'Was your wife making more money than you?'

'She had a full-time job, if that's what you mean.'

'That makes sense. That's the only way the dynamic changes. If the woman is working the same as the man, then there's only common ground and the guy has no room for argument, no leg to stand on. It was different for me. Once I gave up work for Ellie, all duties went my way. He went out and earned the money to afford the roof over our heads, while I fed, watered, mopped up after us all. There were times I would scrub and think, how did I end up in a commercial from the fifties? I hated how I became the good, dutiful wife, looking pretty and keeping house for her husband. It was all such a cliché. Even when Ellie went to preschool and I went back to work part time, I was still earning less, so John pointed out that I should do the lion's share of chores. At the start, I put my point across, saying it over and over, but it never changed. To keep the peace, I carried on, but I'm sure some resentment must have come through. He must have felt it sometimes. I must have pushed him away.'

Niall shook his head, not taking his eyes from me. I hated how he looked at me then, as if he felt sorry for me.

'Peggy, when I said my wife had a full-time job, I meant she stayed at home with the kids. No other job would allow no time for bathroom breaks, especially where a little human follows you in while you're doing your business. Even at a minimum wage job, you're entitled to an hour's lunch break. The lack of sleep, the inability to catch some free time. It's the hardest job in the world.'

My face burned at his answer, at how he must see me now after the question, and I thanked the darkness for shielding my redness and the cold for cooling my skin. Buying time, I flicked my ash aside, and taking another puff, I gathered my thoughts. 'I never saw it that way. It was me who felt lucky because I got to stay at home when he had to leave and go to work. It is a hard job, but it is also the most rewarding.'

'True. I had the opposite problem. When I came home, I would feel guilty seeing the dark circles under my wife's eyes, and I would try to make the light come back in them. I would scoop the kids up and get them outside and give her a moment to sit or shower or do whatever she wanted. I would bring home take out and yes, I would change nappies when needed. We are not all neanderthals, you know?'

I dropped my head, picked at a bobble of wool on my coat. 'I'm sorry I said that. It was wrong of me. I shouldn't have assumed. When you live a certain way for a long time, you believe it's normal.' I nudged him. 'Where were you when I needed you, huh?'

He leaned into the nudge and rested his head on mine. 'I'd like to be there for you now if you'd let me.'

I didn't argue or encourage, just took in that moment, of feeling another person against me, telling me he cared.

After Niall manoeuvred us back to the safety of the airport without mishap, we settled in the welcome warm terminal, the floor not seeming as hard when there were three warmer smiles to sit next to. None of us spoke, waiting for what was coming. Donal topped up the four brandy glasses, and I took mine greedily after being outside in the cold.

'We lost our first child five years ago,' Donal said.

I almost dropped the brandy glass.

'Something inside me has never recovered. He wasn't yet five months, long enough to love him, but not long enough for the hospital to class him as a baby. They call it a miscarriage instead of a stillborn. Miscarriage.'

He blew out his breath.

'There's guilt stuffed into that word. Blame. Like the woman mislaid what she was carrying, or the baby, fetus, made a mistake and decided not to be born. But he had been a real-life person to us. We'd called him Reggie, and I used to lie with my face on my wife's stomach and speak to him every night before bed. Until the night a sound that could only be pain, a roar that made me jump from the bed still asleep, woke me. And then the sight of her, her legs covered in blood, my baby losing our baby, her blood mixed with his blood dripping onto our bedroom carpet.'

Donal choked up.

'Never in my whole life will I forget that sight and there I was, helpless, able to do nothing but sit beside her, drive her to the hospital, while she was bent over crying, us both knowing we were losing Reggie. How can you lose someone you've never met?' He rubbed at his face and Aidan beside him patted his back.

'Let it out, man,' he said.

Donal rubbed at his face until it was dry. The airport had quietened now; most people had given up the fight to stay awake and down the line, all I could see were lumps and curled up bodies in various positions of sleep.

'It took a long time to get over it. Funny how life goes, though, isn't it? The very thing we thought we wouldn't cope with, her best friend's pregnancy, turned how we felt about it to positive again. Caught up in all the excitement, Tracy begged me to try again. Two times we lost our babies in the first six weeks, that's only enough time to find out, two weeks of celebration, only to have the bleeding start. The miscarriage was barely seen, the bloody mass not enough to decipher what our baby's sex, checking the bathroom and wondering did we accidentally flush him or her. There wasn't enough time for them to form, or even to tell anyone, to celebrate but each one reinforced that I just wasn't meant to have children.'

He lifted his hands in front of him, examining them. They were calloused and big.

'I'm good with my hands. I can make almost anything from stuff hanging around. Tracy, even through grief, still tried to help me, even though each loss broke the woman more, watching what she had to go through, what her body had to go through, I don't think I could have done it but that's my wife for you.'

He smiled at the thought of her.

'She's so strong, a million times stronger than me. She suggested I make something in their memory and that idea saved me from going insane. Each time we lost a baby I built something in the garden, my variation of a gravestone, knowing it couldn't take the pain away, but I wanted a physical thing, a marker. It was the least I could do after the happiness we'd felt having them for the moment. I needed to make a reminder that they existed, cos they didn't get to make their own memories. For Reggie, I built a birdhouse and when I say birdhouse, I'm not talking about some little wooden one that will wear away. This one is magnificent.'

Donal's proud grin threatened to take over his entire face.

'It'll stand the test of time, and I hope when I go, it is beautiful enough for whoever takes over my house to want to keep it. I made it from bits of stone and pebbles stacked on top of each other and smoothed out, not random pieces, but the perfect ones. I looked everywhere for the right shapes, only the best would do for Reggie.'

'That's love, Donal,' I said.

He nodded. 'That is what it was, pure love. We gave our two other angels names that could have been for a boy or a girl, Charlie and Jo. For Charlie, I dug out the bottom of the garden and stacked rocks on the hill, and hid a pump in between, so it made a water feature that trickled into a pond. I spent weeks planning it and designing it, learning how far you have to dig, so, if the water freezes, there would be enough water underneath for fish to survive. Lined it, put sand down. Researched the best plants to grow inside so the fish could eat them. The motion of it helped me. With each stone laid, I felt myself get stronger. Once done, I filled it with Koi. For Jo, I built a rocking chair with a roof of slatted wood that I surrounded by a metal trellis. It took me months, but I made something that will stand the test of time. I wanted somewhere to sit and think of them, somewhere me and Tracy could sit in the rain and rock and watch the birds and fish and remember. When Tracy lost the fourth baby, at four months, I sat on that rocking chair and spoke to my children and promised them I would have no more, that I wouldn't put my wife or them through any more pain. I couldn't bring myself to make anything else.'

'Oh Donal, I'm so sorry,' I said, a tear rolling down my cheek.

Donal contemplated his glass and drained it.

'I'm sorry, too,' Niall said. 'Losing one child must have been hard, four would break any person.'

'That's rough,' Aidan said, wiping at his eyes. Aidan acted tough, but he had already proved that anger, in most cases, is only a way of hiding pain.

'After that, I told Tracy I couldn't do it anymore, and she agreed. We booked me in for a vasectomy and planned the rest of our lives. We discussed adoption, but everything seemed forced. Our hearts weren't in any of it. There was a gap between us we couldn't undo, and I knew it was because we were failures, because each time we looked at each other, it reminded us of what we lost. And of what we failed to do. Once I realised this, I knew I couldn't lose Tracy as well. Back when we were trying, we saved for a baby fund, in case we ever needed IVF. The problem wasn't getting pregnant though, it was keeping them with us. I convinced Tracy we needed to spend it on just us two, so we booked a two-month trip, a once in a lifetime holiday we labelled *the holiday we couldn't have with a baby*, and we lived it up. Tracy suggested we write a list of things we could do without children. A kind of bucket list, things that would be a nightmare with kids. We took a cookery course in Italy, we spent two weeks in the Maldives scuba diving around bright coloured fish, and we healed, you know? In India, we got the dreaded Delhi belly. When Tracy's vomiting didn't end after we arrived home, we got worried, thinking she may have some parasite or something, and went to the doctor together. When he announced we were pregnant, I dropped Tracy's hand. Only for the fact we had spent every waking hour in each other's company for two months, I wouldn't have believed the baby was mine but he explained, a vasectomy isn't always effective. He offered to do tests, but I didn't need to. In my heart, I knew I was the father.'

'Oh my,' I said, my hands going to my face in shock.

'I don't know whether it was because of the closeness we regained on that trip, or because the baby was an absolute miracle, or maybe we just relaxed. Whatever it was, something felt different to us from the day we found out. I still worried and watched Tracey like a hawk, yet as each month passed, we grew a little more confident. Too confident. Because that, my friends, is why I'm here.'

Donal poured another brandy into his glass and held it up in offering to the rest of us. Aidan shook his head, still holding his untouched last drink. I refused, still having half mine left. Niall held up his glass and Donal poured. It took forever.

'Oh, come on, finish and tell us,' I said.

Donal took a sip and savoured it before speaking again. 'Tracy has researched every single thing about birth you can imagine. Home births, hypnobirthing, water pools. I understood but put my foot down on the home birth because if anything happened, I needed her to be in a place that could deal with an emergency. Even though the pregnancy has been a dream, we bought nothing baby wise for the house, an old wives' tale I think, not to bring anything in until the baby is born. Whatever it is, even though neither of us are superstitious, even though we'd laugh at those things, we didn't dare. Fast forward to last Sunday night and Tracy sat up in the bed and I thought the worst, thinking something was wrong. She told me we couldn't have a birth without a rebozo, which is a shawl used in Mexico to help with birth. Apparently, you wrap it around the stomach and it can help and guide the baby. I reassured her, telling her we would get it, we could make up a shawl, wanting to get her back to sleep, but in the morning, she was obsessed, and it wouldn't leave her. No matter what I said, I couldn't convince her that any shawl would do. Tracy had to have one of these. It was like the future of our baby depended on it. When I could see how much it was stressing her out, instead of fighting her, I did everything I could to find one. My research found one in Kent, and I went to pay for postage, but Tracy wouldn't have it saying the Christmas post had stopped so we wouldn't get it for weeks and then it would be too late. I looked at this woman who was acting crazy and I could see how scared she was and what she needed me to do to fix it and even though my wife was eight and a half months pregnant, even though everything in me resisted going, I got on the next flight to England.'

'She was nesting,' I said.

Donal wagged his finger at me. 'See, Peggy, I wish you had been with us before I booked the flight. We could have done with that little insight. All went well with the journey. I rang Tracy every hour, or she sent me texts back. It was an in and out journey. Arrived early yesterday morning before talk of any snow falling. We thought we were clever checking the weather for Cork, but didn't think there would be a difference in Stansted. Who knew the snow would come? Oblivious at that stage, I got the train into London where the man met me and we exchanged the rebozo for cash. I had enough time to duck into that famous shop for a cheeky secret present for Tracy and was back on the train and in Stansted for lunchtime. And then dear folks, we all know what happened and it would have been the end of my story until I made a phone call to her when you all went for a break. Tracey's having pains, and it looks like this time they're not Braxton Hicks. There's a rhythm to them and they aren't going away. She's booked a taxi, and she's going to the hospital right away. I can hear the worry that I'm not there, and I'm worried too because I don't want to miss it, and the guilt I feel now is unbelievable because it's my fault that she's scared and alone.'

'Don't do that to yourself Donal, Tracy wanted you to go,' Aidan said.

'But I should have known not to take a risk. The whole pregnancy we've been careful and then we go and make a stupid decision like leaving. What if we broke our lucky bond?'

'How long gone is she?' I asked.

'She was due end of Jan.'

'Many a baby has been born at that age and thrived.'

'You think so?' Donal's question hung in the air and I answered with a confidence I didn't believe, but I knew what he needed to get through the night until he could get on a plane home to his wife.

'She's in safe hands. The hospital will know what to do and, look it, you could have another miracle soon. A Christmas baby and you a new father,' I said.

'I think we should vote. While the stories are fresh in our head.'

Aidan put up his hand. 'I'll vote but I'm telling you now, count me out of the running.'

We all started to protest, but Aidan stabbed the air with his hand higher. 'I've sat here and listened to your stories. You all have actual problems.'

'Aidan, your problems are real,' Niall said.

'They are. To me, they are. The me before, the me even with Nancy, would have listed all the reasons I should get on the flight or why I'm more entitled or important. The me before wouldn't have even entertained you. I would have told you go away, that I was second in line and that was it and if Donal had insisted on listening, I would have insisted on changing places with him and going first. And then I listened to you all. Now, here I am and I've just realised I don't need to get on that plane to be happy. For the first time in my life, I sat down with three strangers and told them my story and they seemed, anyway, to accept me as I am. And you know what? I'm all right as I am. Don't get me wrong, I'll still go to Nancy and tell her everything, but it doesn't have to be on the very next plane. That ticket, my ticket, is going to one of you.' He turned to Niall. 'I'm sorry, but I'm going to vote for Peggy and Donal. Donal can't miss his child's birth, simple as. And Peggy, well, I grew up without a mother that cared about me, and every year all I wished for was for her to show up and love me. I would have given away every toy, given away anything, to be held by her at Christmas. I also know how you can survive without a mother. You'll be all right. For that reason, I think it should be Peggy that goes.'

'I agree,' Niall said.

'I don't,' I said.

Niall laughed. 'Well, hold on there and let a guy speak. I had many chances to repair the relationship with my mother, and I never took it. We made mistakes and I live by the consequences. I could get on that plane and learn she died or I could arrive there and it be the same as it always was, her mouth clamped and me worse for it. What will be, will be. Your daughter depends on you, needs you at Christmas and something like this could damage the relationship. Ellie will only remember you broke your promise.'

'Only if I don't get back for Christmas morning. Even if that happened,

I would make it up to her. I would make sure she understood I did everything I could to get home.'

'It doesn't work like that. Look at me, Peggy,' Niall said. He looked at me like he was searching for something in my eyes. I wasn't sure if he was looking for an answer or hoping for me to convince him. 'The reason I'm in this mess is because of what happened to me as a child. My vote goes to you two. The little girl who is waiting for her mummy and the other who is about to be born and needs his or her daddy. Donal and Peggy.'

'Well, I want to vote for Niall and Donal, and I'll tell you why,' I said.

'Hold on.' Donal said. 'Looks to me like I have the casting vote. Before you argue, let me tell you how I'm voting. I think it should be Niall and Peggy, although after hearing from Tracy I won't argue with you if you want to give me your ticket. I will take it and wish that I could get there right now.'

'It's decided then. Three votes for Donal and Peggy and two for Niall. Sorry Niall,' Aidan said.

Niall looked away, trying to hide his welling eyes by moving his hand to his hair. 'It's the right decision.'

I chewed down on my lip, wanting to argue, but the image of Ellie without me held me back. I was desperate to get to her. As the guys fell into other conversation, more to distract I think than anything, as Donal spoke about possible names, I tried to work out a way that everyone could get what they wanted this Christmas. Over and over, I tried every different scenario and when I could come up with nothing; I went to the last resort: I made a silent plea, and asked, begged more like, whoever was in charge, for a miracle.

Donal raised his glass and said, 'I would like to make a toast, to Christmas wishes. We all have them, and I wish that every one of ours comes true.'

We all touched glasses, clinked, looked at each other straight in the eye and said, 'To Christmas Wishes.'

After that, there wasn't much point in conversation. They decided, and judging from the dark circles under each of the men's eyes, the day had exhausted them. We fell asleep side by side, huddled together, the excuse being there wasn't enough room between the ticket desk and the vomit, but in my case, I needed the comfort of someone else next to me. In a lit up, artificial, hard floored, bleach smelling, semi-clean airport floor, I slept like a baby wedged in between three guys.

On that floor, I had a dream where I sat on the same bench as earlier that morning, but this time there was a gigantic clock suspended from the patterned ceiling. It was a mechanical one, its face displaying the intricate cogs that turn the time. I watched the hands move and the cogs turn, picking up speed and going faster and faster. It was the sound, though, that got to me. Every time the hand moved it sounded like a tut, each one a reprimand, reminding me to atone, reminding me as each second moved on I was losing time and wasting what was left.

Tut. Tut. Tut.

Morning

The airport stirring woke me and when I opened my crusty and still tired eyes from only catching a few hours' sleep, I wondered how we ever slept through the lights turning on. It was the brandy. Coupled with the stale cigarette which formed a film on my tongue, both left their mark with a slight hum in my head. I checked my watch, twenty to five. There was no one appointed to our counter yet, but the bustle around the terminal told me it wouldn't be much longer. The gap in the window above us still showed black and was no good at letting me know whether the weather had turned during the night. The others were still asleep and I let them, wanting a minute to gather my thoughts and run through the goings on. Niall's eyes screwed up while he slept, as if in the middle of a nightmare, or in pain. He had a gentle face. A face that held open eyes when awake and had so far acted trustworthy. I learnt more about these men in a few hours than ten dinner dates with John. He always said I saw the good in everyone. I used to respond that I liked to see the good, that my doing so made even the not so good ones want to be better in my presence, even if only for a moment.

Had John been one of the not so good ones? The problem with only seeing the good in people was when they hurt me, they took me lower than I thought was possible.

I knew the check in assistant was for us before she reached the desk. The woman wore a pair of Christmas stocking earrings dangling from her ears and was dressed as Mrs Claus. I rolled my eyes. The last thing we needed was some dope. There was a saunter to her walk, a jolliness I didn't feel. She walked like she knew it was going to be a good day and despite my reservations, the heaviness in my chest lifted some bit.

Careful not to wake the others, I stood and rubbed the sleep from my eyes and approached her. 'Sorry, I know you haven't started yet, but can I ask, what will happen to the others in the airport, the ones that won't make the flight?'

The woman stopped by the congealed vomit and screwed up her nose at the still asleep man surrounded by it. 'Tough night?' she asked me.

'Enlightening,' I said.

'I'd say it was,' she said, holding her nose as she moved on.

'Will we all get home?'

The woman tsked at the question. 'I'll do my best. The good news is the snow isn't due to fall until this afternoon, so once the sun rises, we should have some melting and the visual to get rid of the snow. There's extra staff coming in too. Now move and let me do my job.' She slid past me. 'I can't see what's available until I check the computer.'

I woke the guys one by one with just a slight rub on each of their shoulders. They rose without trouble, which was more than could be said for Rugby fella, nudged awake by two security guards. Judging by the pointed fingers from the many disgruntled people that formed a circle around the men, they were filling them in that he had skipped the queue.

The now hungover man looked sheepish and small, not the bullish brute full of bravado anymore. 'That's karma,' I said.

The words were no sooner out of my mouth when they hit me. Karma. The sum of someone's actions decided their fate in the future. I believed in it without question, so what was I doing?

'Come on now. Wakey Wakey, if you want to get home, we have to get this line moving.' The woman called in a singsong tone.

Home. There was that word again. Calling me. I thought about what home meant to me. How it wasn't just made up of Ellie. My mother was home, too.

Donal stepped up to be the first in line, but stopped to allow me to move ahead. I shook my head.

'I can't do it. You need to go, Niall.'

Niall was ashen and looked like sleep hadn't helped him. Still, he shook his head. I stepped behind him.

'Guys, I know you're having some kind of domestic here, but can you do it after? I have to get this show on the road if you want to get home.'

I waved at Donal to take the spot. Once he started talking to Mrs Claus, I turned to Niall.

'All of you made the wrong choice last night. It shouldn't have been me that got the ticket. Death and birth, they are things a son or daughter or a father should never miss. They are the moments that if you do, bring a lifetime of regret.'

Niall looked pained. 'I can't, Peggy. Your daughter.'

'Look at me Niall,' he did as told, and I could see as before, he hoped I could convince him to accept what he was desperate for.

'At the end of it all, you are still a son that needs his mother. I will find a way home to Ellie. It may take a couple of extra hours, but my daughter will have me for the rest of my life. Your mother needs you for the rest of hers. You need to say goodbye, Niall.'

Niall let out two breaths, forcing the emotion away. As he did, his shoulders slumped, and he gave up the resistance, and the skin on his face slid into pained wrinkles. 'I do, don't I?'

'This way we can all still get our Christmas wish,' I whispered as I hugged him.

'Are you sure?' He whispered back.

'More than anything in my entire life,' I said.

He burrowed his head into my neck, and I could hear his voice catching as he spoke.

Aidan came up behind us, placing a gentle palm on my shoulder. 'You need to go, Niall.'

'All of you have given me the greatest gift.' Niall said, openly crying. 'Not just you giving me this spot, Peggy. What you've said. Meeting you. Last night with all you... I feel differently about, about everything, if that makes sense?'

'It does. I feel it, too.'

Niall pulled back to look at me.

'The plane won't wait, you know?' The woman called out. We broke apart.

'Go on Niall. Let yourself see your mother. Say all the things you need to say, listen to all you need to hear. Let it heal.'

Instead of moving on, Donal stood to the side, waiting for us. I looked at each of those men. 'From the sound of it, we've all been hard on ourselves. From today we need to stop that.'

Niall approached the counter with a lighter step than the day before, a step that said he was ready, excited even to get on the plane. Donal scooted over and nudged my side as I watched the back of Niall with tears in my eyes. Because when it came down to it, even though I knew I had done the right thing, I hadn't chosen my daughter.

'You did the right thing there,' Donal said.

'I did, didn't I?' I mumbled.

'According to Alicia here, she's going to get everyone home. There are flights still available for Shannon and Dublin, Peggy. You are still going to get there.'

I couldn't stop my face from crumpling. Not a good look, but I didn't care. 'I am?'

He smiled. 'You are. It'll be a bit of a longer journey, but what if you and Aidan hired a car and drove together?'

I turned to Aidan. 'Fancy taking a spin with me?'

Aidan laughed a full on, open-mouthed laugh, and his face lifted. 'Looks like I'm going to Cork to make a fool of myself then.'

I rubbed his arm. 'If it doesn't turn out, you're more than welcome to have Christmas in mine.'

'Sounds like a plan,' he said.

'Why aren't you running off?' I asked Donal.

'Not boarding for another hour. They are clearing the runway as we speak.'

Once Niall finished, he stood beside Donal, waiting for us.

'So, where are you sending me?' I asked as I approached the woman.

The woman tsked, her earrings rocking. 'Well now, where do you want to go?'

I looked back at the long line of people. 'What will happen to the others who need a flight?'

'Depends on what they're looking for. They're working on opening the train lines and sending some to Heathrow. It means going further than your destination. I can offer Shannon, Knock and Dublin. All the crew have said they will work on. If we need to do another run, they will. Whatever it takes. If I have my way, there won't be no one left in this airport that doesn't want to be here.' Alicia stopped, tsked again at my expression. 'Come on now, you didn't think we would keep you all here for Christmas, did you?'

Glimmer

I stood next to the two men to wait for Aidan and pulled out my phone to ring my mother and tell her the good news when a message beeped.

Please tell me you're still stranded and get to come back to me.

Instead of feeling a glimmer of hope, the text irked me. John would be glad if I missed Christmas with our daughter. His first concern was about him, not her.

I reread the many texts he had sent the last few days, and I stopped at the lines *before Ellie*. Reruns of old conversations played back in my mind.

'Do you really want a baby?'

'Course I do. We planned this, remember?' My back straightening up, rubbing my baby bump, on alert now.

'Course, I'm just checking on you, that's all.'

I read the text over and over.

when you became a mum, I lost a wife... I could ask anything of you and you'd do it... I was your everything.

He had been my everything because I had put him above all else, including any want of mine. I thought now of all the times I pushed down my preferences and put his needs to the forefront, knowing it would make life easier, not causing an argument, not wanting a debate, choosing the easy way out.

Donal caught my shoulder and pulled at Aidan's sleeve.

'Come on, before we separate, I want to show ye something.'

'We have to board.'

'We have some time. Come on, it will be worth it.'

He led us to the other side of the airport. 'Ah,' I said, realising what he was doing.

'Alicia told me they cleared arrivals already,' Donal said.

People stood around. Some dressed with Christmas hats or tinsel around their necks. Some held signs, some shifted from side to side with excitement. And then the glass doors slid open and the first passengers pushed trolleys through and the sound erupted in the arrival hall. And people broke barriers and abandoned luggage and rushed into each other. One little girl ran the length of the airport and jumped into the arms of a grey-haired woman. Before I knew it, I was a sobbing mess. The air in the arrivals terminal grew lighter, where only a few hours ago it was full of fear and unknowing it was now replaced with something much more welcome. Surrounded by Christmas trees and tinny Christmas songs were people with tears flowing, thankful people who knew how grateful they should be for having the chance to spend Christmas with their loved ones. Whether it was because it was Christmas, or because of the ordeal they had faced, the people didn't hold back their joy at seeing each other, and the sight of that filled me with hope.

'That will be us in a couple of hours,' Niall whispered to me.

I turned to him and, caught up by the love in the room, surprised us both by kissing him on the lips. I pulled away, mortified, and reddened at what I'd just done.

'I'm sorry, Niall, I shouldn't have just done that. You have enough to worry about with going to your mother and everything is still up in the air with John. I shouldn't have feelings still.' I stopped, the words out loud held clarity now I said them. 'But I still do, and it wouldn't be fair to get involved.'

'I'd settle for friends,' he said, nudging me on the shoulder with his own. 'As long as you know it would be settling. Until you're ready, I mean.'

'What if I get back with him?'

'Then you haven't led me on. I think there could be something special between us, and I'd like to get to know you, Peggy. I haven't felt this pull towards anyone for a very long time and if it doesn't go anywhere, I'll still be glad I met you.'

'Friends then, for now,' I said, putting out my hand to shake his.

'For now,' he said, pushing away my hand and giving me a full on hug instead. As I melted into his touch, I found it felt different from the night I embraced John, when the happiness blended with pain and regret and heartbreak. This hug was full of hope and promise and felt warm and safe and as I nuzzled into his neck, I noticed he smelt fantastic for someone who had slept on the floor and before I could even stop myself, I had found his lips again and kissed him. It wasn't a snog, or a friendly peck, but a slight open-mouthed touch of the lips that promised I wanted more, my body contradicting my words. When I broke away, Niall's eyes were closed, and he was smiling.

'Now that's my kind of friend.'

'I shouldn't have done that. I'm sorry. Again.'

'Why? Don't feel guilty. I'm under no illusion, Peggy. You may or may not get back with your husband. If so, I just got a kiss from a beautiful woman on Christmas Eve. If that is all it ever turns out to be, that was enough to make me smile, especially with how the rest of my day is going to go. Isn't that what a friend does?'

'That was what it was, a friendly kiss,' I said, laughing.

'You just did what I wished I had the courage to do,' he said. Then waved as we went our separate ways.

Snippets

We drove in silence most of the way home. It was a mutual non-talking, an amiable quiet. Having spent the flight chatting, we awarded each other a tranquil allowance to become lost in our own thoughts, to plan what needed to be done. I ran through lists of food I needed to prepare, presents I needed to wrap. It was too late for Miss Rainbow, all shops closed early in Ireland on Christmas Eve and I resolved to writing some kind of note to Ellie that Santa would drop it to her another day. Miss Rainbow didn't matter. Nothing else mattered. Not presents. Not money. Not the best seats on the flight. Not what clothes I wore. Not even the gift of a father. Nothing mattered except holding my girl when she opened her eyes. Love was all that counted.

We passed lit up houses, signs asking for Santa to stop there. On our own private journey, wishing time would go faster but also stop or wait for us to get there. I wished for a Christmas miracle for Niall and Donal. That a mother would hold on until words could be said, words that needed to be heard and that another friend got to hold a hand as new life broke through into this world.

Flashes of my previous life came to me on that journey. Snippets of the truth that I had taken at the time and hidden in corners of my mind came to the surface now. The sound of texts that beeped on John's phone that made him jump from the sofa next to me as if he'd dropped something hot on himself. How he would walk into the kitchen to reply, yet when he went to the bathroom, there would be no sign of a text. Erased. And I let my mind do the same as his thumbs; I swiped it from my memory.

Or how he stopped looking at me. Or looked differently. It changed, the eyes once full of lust or admiration or love, became ambivalent side glances, as if he knew me so well he didn't have to look right at me, that there was no surprise, that he'd seen all he needed to see.

I saw now all the things that had been in plain sight then, but I either didn't see or didn't want to see. The hesitation between the words. I thought I knew that man's quirks and wishes because he always agreed with me. We never argued. Being honest, I knew he wasn't happy, not really, even though he always said he was, reassured me when I asked, but I'd knew the buzz had gone from him. I booked nights out for us to bring the spark back where we could dress up and talk and do fun, adult things but it was like someone put a jinx on us and either the babysitter would cancel or Ellie would get sick and I would feel the disappointment of that, I would lie in bed cradling her while she coughed or vomited and John slept in the spare room and wondered what I could have done, how I could change things. Because I could feel the split between us even then, I could feel the divide, the need to divide my attention between my baby and my husband and one of them always fell short.

But he had been the one to choose to look elsewhere. He had been the one to cheat. To choose someone else instead of sorting what he should have done. It was his fault, not mine.

This new found anger felt satisfying, but even as I thought it, I still knew I wasn't free from blame. I had withdrawn from him. Ellie became everything, but wasn't that what happened? That the mother got lost for a while looking after her baby because without her the baby wouldn't survive. That the mother came back to the father if he gave her the opportunity and if he did, the love was stronger. I thought we were partners, weathering life together side by side.

Why had I flown to John the moment he made contact? As much as I liked to pretend it was all for Ellie, most of it had been for me, to have a warm body, a male body, hold me. I ran to him in the hope I could have my image of family back, the three of us home. But on the drive, I allowed myself to remember what that meant. The truth. Life had been late nights waiting for him to come home, with him going straight to bed, announcing his exhaustion. It was dinners not eaten, with bills for expensive restaurants chosen instead. Or his bored expression as I told him about my day. It was competing with the back of a phone. The smirks from women at his work when I dropped something off. Somewhere, over the years, I had lost the person who I had believed was my husband, and it left me with someone I didn't know anymore. And the lightning bolt idea flashed before me as we stopped at a traffic light. The truth was, I didn't want to.

As we neared Knockfarraig, my thoughts turned to Ellie. An excitement bubbled as the roads veered into my road and by the time Aidan pulled up at my house, I couldn't wait to say goodbye to him, opening the car door before he stopped. I was out before he said a word, shouting to him, 'Best of luck. Call me after and whatever happens, come back and stay here. OK?'

All worries about John left me and I ran up my drive and the door opened and there she was, the beacon, the representation of home, my little girl, my Ellie, with that big grin of hers, and her unrestrained excitement at seeing me, with my mother behind, clasping her hands to her face, and tears down her cheeks and everything other than that moment faded. And then she was in my arms and I smelt her again and touched her hair and cried into her neck and breathed her in and there she was, a real live thing. I couldn't believe I had done it. I had kept my promise and got home. Picking Ellie up, I carried her into the warm house. My mother rubbed my back as I walked and as all three of us sat on the couch to hug each other, I felt my heart would burst at being given the best Christmas present I could ever ask for.

* * *

As I scooped up the last bit of wrapping from the living room, I took a sip from my glass. I had prepped the food; wrapped the presents, and read and sang to my exhausted daughter. Before my mother had called it a night, she had poured me a much needed glass of wine, and now, I sat alone, transfixed at the sparkling Christmas lights. I thought about Ellie and how much she was going to love Christmas day, how that smile of hers would spread wide enough to see every tooth as she opened her presents. I thought about Niall and how he said he used to help his wife and how John had stepped back from all that. If he had been here now, if he had never left, it would have still been me preparing the room alone. Finding presents and decorating trees were all my issues. Now I was alone, and for the first time since he left, I was glad of it. I didn't have to answer to him any longer; I didn't have to explain what I was spending on our daughter, going through each itemised receipt as he nodded and scowled, even though money wasn't an issue for us at all. From now on I could encourage her to whoop and have as much fun on the day as possible, not curb her noise or brush over her excitement by giving him as much attention. And there it was, I admitted it: my husband had been jealous of our daughter. I had spent years trying to make sure the both of them were happy.

I got out my phone and, buoyed by the half a glass of wine, not waiting for even a hello, I said what I had to say.

'I'm releasing you, John. I don't want a relationship with you anymore. You are free. You don't have to be a good husband, or at least, my husband, from now on. Live where you want, have the life that you want, with whoever you want. What you have to do, though, what I will hold you accountable for, is being a good father. Which means turning up when you say you will. Getting the toy that you promised you'd get. Being there for her. She needs a father as much as a mother.'

There was silence, and I wondered if I'd just spoken to a dead phone line. I heard an outtake of breath.

'I can do that. It's just... I didn't want to rub your face in it. I was afraid how it would go down if I turned up and wanted to take her somewhere. Imagine your mother's face if I tried to do that.'

It was my turn to take a long breath.

'She wouldn't stop you from seeing Ellie. She wants the same as me which is for you to be there for your daughter. I wouldn't have coped these last couple of months without my mother,' I said it more hotly than I planned.

'You're right, I just meant your mum wasn't my biggest fan.'

I bit my tongue. There were so many things I could say if I wanted to hurt him. He had given her plenty of reason to doubt him. For years, she had told me I was a fool.

I held back because none of those things would help the situation. Most of all, I held back because there was no reason to say it anymore; I wouldn't change him and just then I laughed, because I realised I'd given up the fight and the want to keep him. My husband's affairs and issues were now someone else's problem. Speaking to the guys, I had seen everyone carries their own problems, including John. I would never understand how he could have acted that way with me, but for the first time, I believed I deserved better than what he'd ever offered me. It wasn't even about being with Niall, or the opportunity to have something with Niall. What he had done was lift a mirror up to my relationship with John, so I could see it wasn't real, and that other types of love existed. No more would I settle for scraps of love, clawing at the remnants of what it should be. Being on my own was better, and because of that, I felt lighter than I had in years.

'Here's a suggestion. Why don't you book a flight in the New Year and check in to a hotel or something? I mean, maybe later on you could stay at the house, in the spare room, but I don't think I'm ready for that yet.

And John?'

'Yeah?'

'No girlfriend. Not this time.'

'Understood. Hold on,' he said. There was a muffling sound on the phone followed by some tapping noises. I exhaled.

'There's a flight available on Monday. I'll still be on holidays until the fourth so I could stay a few days if that's all right with you? I could bring Ellie out to make up for missing Christmas.'

'That's what we'll do then,' I said.

'Peggy?'

'Yeah?'

'Thank you.'

'Happy Christmas John.'

'Happy Christmas Peggy.'

Christmas Wishes

She reached for Niall's hand, and her own felt cold and bony. 'You came,' she said.

She closed her eyes and for a moment he thought she would take her last breath, but she pursed her lips together, moving them from side to side, as if she was trying to moisten them or the action would help her find the words. When she opened her eyes, she looked straight at him. 'I'm sorry. I did it all wrong.'

'Mum, stop, it's all right,' he said, stroking her hand with his thumb.

'Shh,' she said, closing her eyes again, slipping away for a moment. There wasn't another sound in the room, and Niall thought he had never concentrated so much or waited for a next word. She edged closer, lifting her neck to him as if she was mustering all her strength. He propped her up with an extra pillow, waiting for her to get comfortable, noticing the winces as she moved. It pained him to see the deterioration in her, the hollowed bones, the dark circles, the life leaving her skin. Her vibrancy that he always took for granted, wiped away now, and he wanted it back. He wanted his mother back.

'I didn't know his name. I told others it was Barry, Barry Keenan, but that was just a name from a newspaper.' She wheezed and only spoke again once her breathing settled. 'He helped a woman. He pushed her to safety… the car killed him.' She closed her eyes again, regained her strength. 'That's the man you should have had. The kind you deserved.'

She smacked her lips together, and Niall reached for the water on her bedside locker and she sipped at it once, then pushed it away. He could tell she was eager to go on, that the fight was leaving her, and she needed to get it all out. 'I could tell others of a dead hero...' she reached for Niall's hand again, 'I could never have lied to you. It was better to say nothing until it was too late to say anything. It meant losing you.' She gulped. 'It was still better than the truth. I never wanted you to carry it.' She closed her eyes again, and the lines beside them filled with tears.

'I don't want to hear it, mum. It's OK now, I understand.'

It was the truth. In those words that were said, Niall heard enough.

'I didn't come for that. There was a time I thought I did. For years, I believed I needed to know. What I needed was to understand, and now I do. There's nothing more you need to say about that. What I need, what I came to say to you, is I'm sorry.'

His own breath caught then.

'Because I took your love and made you feel like it was less than it was when really it was everything. You did nothing wrong, nothing at all. I'm sorry for pushing you away. Know that I don't blame you. Please know that.'

She placed her other hand on top of the hand that was stroking hers. 'My boy,' she said.

Her breathing became more ragged, and there were no more words spoken from her. The need to speak or fight or open her eyes left her and the rest of the night became a series of gargles and noises, the breath becoming harder to grasp onto. He held her hand and nodded at the friends and relations who joined him, glad of their company, of being around his kin, his own blood, the same blood running through the veins of the only ones left that mattered. Strength came from having them in the room, which gave a rhythm to it, the old people knowing the ways of death, knowing what the noises signified, understanding what little time his mother had left. Although appreciated, their company faded into the background. They were just there, acknowledged yet half noticed, because it was only his mother that Niall saw. He spoke to her in whispers, telling her how he loved her, reminding her of stories he had kept close in his heart, of all the moments he had etched in his memory, of the love she had given him, of the fact that she gave enough love to be a father and a mother. In telling those stories, while holding her hand, Niall felt a warmness spread in his chest, close to the same feeling he got while drinking the brandy the night before, when he told three strangers a story and they had shared their own with him, and after that, left as friends.

Between the early hours of when Christmas Eve met Christmas morning, the suffering left Doris, all traces of the pain that savaged her went, and with it, the life of her drained from her face, smoothing out the lines and the pinching around her mouth softened and her lips became slack. Niall knew the exact second she left him. A contradiction of emotions ran through. Relief that she wasn't in pain any longer, shock from thinking he would have more time. A grief wrenched inside his chest that dug in so deep he didn't know if he would ever get over it. Alongside all that sorrow, he felt a gratitude stronger than he had ever experienced, thankful for so many things - the exchange of a place from a woman who had won it fair and square. For an angry man who cast his own needs aside, for the sake of another. Thankful for a guy at the top of a line, that didn't have to listen. The plane that brought him to his mother. For everything Doris had ever done for him. Most of all, he was thankful for the chance to say goodbye, and for a Christmas wish come true.

Tiptoes

The phone beeped in the middle of the night and bleary-eyed, a picture lit up the screen with an image of a baby, all puffy and swollen with the remnants of the amniotic sac, milky white still on its face.

I had never seen a more beautiful sight.

Another message beeped. *Got there in time, thanks to you all. Still in the dog house though, but I told Tracy I have a lifetime to make it up to her! Meet Holly, 7lbs 2 ounces, born 12.03 Christmas day and already the love of our life!*

My thumbs worked slow across the keypad, still half asleep, *She is beautiful. The best present you could ever hope for. She was born with the veil! That's good luck. If Tracey is staying in the hospital, you are welcome to some grub in mine later (or to wet the baby's head. I owe you a brandy!)*

As the night turned to dawn, my phone beeped again and knowing it was just a response to my last text, sleep tempted me to ignore it. I didn't recognise the number. It was one line.

I'm outside.

I tiptoed downstairs, careful to not wake Ellie. Standing next to my car was Aidan, looking sheepish and cold, with his hands burrowed into his jean pockets and a bag on the floor.

'I'm sorry for it being so early.'

I grabbed him and gave him a big bear hug, then ushered him inside. I put my finger to my mouth, urging him to be quiet, and pointed to the kitchen. We tiptoed inside.

'How did you get on?' I asked.

He smiled, but the smile held a sadness. 'It's a long story,' he said.

I tapped on a chair at the kitchen table. 'I've got time,' I said.

So, we sat, and he told me.

'I went straight to my wife after dropping you off. She opened the door, and the first thing I saw was a small bump, too small to be anything to do with me.'

My hands went to my mouth. 'Oh, Aidan, I'm sorry.'

Aidan shook his head, trying to hold it together. 'Right then, Peggy, I knew it was the end of us. She was nice enough to hear me out and instead of begging her to come back, I apologised for all the times I had closed up or let her down. Told her about the counselling and how different I saw things now. I wished her a happy Christmas, and that I hoped she was happy and before she even replied, I knew her answer, I could see it staring back at me from the photographs of her and the new man she was with, hanging from the walls, smiling out. She had a new life with me erased, a life that would never involve me and I felt the sadness for that, for what I lost, but I also felt happy for her getting what she had deserved and I told her so. As I left, we hugged, and I asked if she could forgive me, and she told me she did.'

I rubbed his hand and, tapping mine; he whispered. 'I'm parched.'

I jumped up and put the kettle on.

'After leaving Nancy's I drove the rental car back by my old family home, a town I hadn't been to since I was a teen, even when Nancy used to go back, for Christmas or birthdays I'd refuse, not wanting to see my old man. On the drive, I thought about the journey Niall and Donal had to make and how I didn't want it to be too late for them. As I drove through the one street town, the Christmas lights lit up the closing shopfronts. I glanced at the old toy store still owned by Mrs Briggs, and the dress shops that looked like they had frozen in time. I parked outside the town's nativity scene, slap bang in the square, and allowed myself a cry. It was there as I stared at the baby Jesus's crib, at the mother and the father, Mary and Jesus, and the people behind them in the crib hovering proud, like family, that made me think about the people I met in the airport, who made me appreciate my life more than any counselling has done. You all gave me something I hadn't in a long time. You gave me hope, Peggy. Because even though my Christmas wish hasn't come true, what I needed was to be brave and take a chance and still know I was going to be OK.'

I handed him a tea, placing milk and sugar on the counter. 'Cheers,' he said, taking it and stirring the milk in. I sat next to him and waited while he took a drink. 'Nothing beats a cup of tea in the morning,' he said, smiling at me.

'Go on,' I said.

'In the end, I couldn't drive past and knocked on the door of a house I never thought I would visit again. It was later, after the shock of my appearance had settled down in my father, after I ate the stew he offered, we sat around the fire drinking a whiskey. The old man had got frail, and the fight has long gone from him and he seemed sorry even. I explained my marriage was over and it had been no one's fault but my own, and he twisted his fingers and said, "I'd say I had a part to play all right." and I didn't disagree because he had, of course he had.'

Aidan rubbed at his thick stubble and looked at me with watery eyes, his voice breaking with the next bit.

'He kept saying the word sorry over and over and I could tell the man meant it. What surprised me was how much I needed it. I had needed to hear it, Peggy, more than anything else in my whole life.'

He wiped at a tear. I said nothing, not wanting to interrupt, but rubbed at his back to encourage him to carry on.

'There by the fire an old man hugged his old man and for the life of me, I couldn't remember him ever doing that before. For the rest of the night, we sat there, and he told me the goings on from the town. Who had died. Who still lived. He told me Mrs Briggs's daughter, Patricia, moved back, and I smiled at the thought. Patricia was my first love, going out together when we were only fifteen. Her marriage didn't work out, either. She's a solicitor now, travels up to Cork each day to work. My father suggested I visit them over Christmas. I changed the subject, saying I saw Mrs Briggs still had the toy shop. He told me Patricia helped her with that, got her on to new suppliers, so they had all the top of the range stuff now, not the old crap she used to sell. He told me they had caused some commotion in the town earlier that day, with queues out the door for some doll that was sold out. Cleaning up, he said. It got me thinking about Patricia and what I was like as her boyfriend. I'd been different with her. I'd loved her with all my heart, giving her the love I'd craved. It was innocent, and I held nothing back, thinking love could solve my pain. The only light in my dark world. I must have been pretty intense. It all shattered when she broke up with me. Instead of fighting for her, I bottled it up and raged at the world and ran away to the apprenticeship. Each time something didn't work out after that, it added and multiplied and proved how shit life was. Last night I lay in my old bed trying to get to sleep when the text came through from Donal. I kept thinking about him, about how happy he must be to hold Holly, and how Nancy would soon feel the same way, too. What I wanted had changed since being with Patricia. I thought I knew what the future held for us. At fifteen, I'd my whole life planned out, college together, marriage, lots of children. I never got over her.'

'I'm sorry,' I said.

'Don't be. I fell asleep and had a dream that I was standing in front of the nativity crib and Donal took Holly from the crib and offered her to me and as I held her in my hands, I thought how perfect new birth was and the baby looked up at me and even though I know a newborn can't smile, she did, and she looked at me with such love, that I felt this warmness spread over me. I woke up then, and the only way I can describe it is I felt like a different person. Like Holly, I felt I'd just been born. Reborn, more like. As if my life was starting again.'

He grinned at me.

'You look different,' I said, and he did. He looked softer around his edges.

'After that I couldn't sleep, so I ran through all the conversations I had gone over the last few hours, savouring the words, letting the random pieces flit through in the hope they would lull me back to sleep. As I was about to slip back, I heard my father's voice say: *"There were queues out the door earlier for some doll that was sold out everywhere."* I shot out of the bed and knowing the whiskey was still in my system, I ran down the town, not stopping even though my heart was thumping in my chest, knowing that the place was closed and there was no rush but feeling like I had to go fast anyway, because I had to see and there in the dusty window of an ancient toy shop sat a display with Miss Rainbow in it and I sat down on the floor and cried because if I done nothing else this year at least I knew I could make a little girl's dream come true.'

He opened his bag and slid a boxed up, perfect Miss Rainbow across the table to me.

Before I spoke, before I let him speak, I ran out of the kitchen and grabbed my stash of wrapping paper and came back and, quicker than ever before, wrapped the present. I flicked my eyes to Aidan. 'Just in case she wakes, once I have this thing that nearly drove me insane out of the way, I am going to give you the biggest kiss, and then I want an explanation.'

Once done, I crept into the living room again and placed the newly wrapped present at the forefront of the tree, then tiptoed back to the kitchen and wrapped my arms around him.

'You know, I didn't know it, but I had a knot in my stomach at the thought of her waking up without that doll. You, Aidan, are a lifesaver.

How?'

The man who grinned back at me looked younger.

'If it was Mrs Briggs who had answered the door to me in the middle of the night, she would have closed it in my face, but it wasn't. Patricia stood there and even though she held a baseball bat in her hand, expecting someone drunk, she still looked as lovely as what I remembered. She didn't turn me away and listened to my story and snuck the keys from the shop off the hook and we ran like children down the street, a street we kissed on twenty something years before and here I am.'

'I can't thank you enough.' I grabbed his hand and squeezed it. 'Stay here, get some sleep, and have dinner with us later. My mother bought a turkey so big I could feed the street with it.'

'No,' Aidan said. 'My dad thinks I'm still in bed. I can't disappear when I've just returned. I need to see if we can heal it. But I could call later if you like?'

'I would love that.'

* * *

After my daughter discovered Miss Rainbow and ran around the room for ten minutes. After she opened the rest of her presents and we sat down to a feast. After the drama of the day settled and all was well with the world again, three people called to my house and stayed until the early hours. One now motherless and grieving, but hopeful too. One wifeless and sad, but open and forgiven and able to forgive. One exuberant from the new life that surrounded him and the dreams that were about to come. Each one differed from as little as two days before. And I had changed, too. Now accepting being husbandless, happy to let go of a man who could never love me the way I wanted.

I poured a glass of brandy for the four of us and held up my glass to make a toast.

'To all the souls who were once with us,' Niall said.

'To learning how good it is to give,' Aidan said.

'To new life,' Donal said.

'To new friendships and realised dreams and to Christmas wishes that never came true,' I said.

And we all drank to that.

An Exclusive Gift For You.

Want another story?

As a thank you for taking the time to read this book, I want to give you a gift. If you subscribe to the Natasha Karis newsletter, you will get:

The Initiation of Alayne Adams - an uplifting novella.

Torn between partying with her friends and doing the right thing, Alayne's life lacks any direction. Until an altercation leaves her spiralling.

Left with nowhere to turn, Alayne tries to find her way. But an encounter in a library opens up new possibilities and a chance to learn. Can Alayne change or will old habits prove too strong?

The Summer Before - an exclusive novella that cannot be bought anywhere else, giving the story that led Calista to the detention room.

Induction - an exclusive short story you won't find anywhere else.

The Initiates - first chapter

You will also be the first to receive exclusive cover reveals, behind the scenes details and giveaways.

Get it today at: https://www.subscribepage.com/initiation

Enjoy this book? You can make a difference.

Honest reviews of my books help bring them to the attention of other readers. If you enjoyed The Truth Between Us, I would really appreciate if you could spend a few minutes leaving your feedback. Reviews help the buyer understand the 'feel' of the book so your review could be the difference in whether someone picks it up.

My deepest thanks,
Natasha Karis.

About the Author

Natasha Karis lives in Cork, Ireland, and spends her days navigating between writing and raising her three children. She has been known to write with a child on her knee. She writes contemporary, emotional, uplifting stories. Natasha carries a book with her everywhere she goes. Even though she has always been a voracious reader, she wasn't always a writer and has worked as a chiropractic clinic manager, a shoe store manager, and a Dunnes Stores girl.

She is the author of The Breaking of Dawn, The Truth Between Us, The Initiates, The Initiation of Alayne Adams and The Happiness Initiative.

Also by Natasha Karis

The Breaking Of Dawn

An emotional novel about the power in finding your voice.

Dawn Moloney has struggled her whole life with words. Finding it impossible to express her opinion, she spends her days doing what others tell her to. Taken for granted by her boss and friends, she can never find the right way to stand up to them. Nobody takes Dawn seriously, including herself.

Forced to move back to her childhood home after an attack leaves her bruised and broken, Dawn struggles to adjust.

When her mother suggests she try classes at a local centre for the unemployed, she reluctantly agrees. There, she meets Alayne Adams, who prefers to focus more on Dawn rather than what classes she is taking. Talking about herself is Dawn's worst nightmare, but if she wants to get better, she will have to learn.

Sometimes you have to step into the darkness to find your light, but can Dawn dive in and finally find the right words?

Although part of The Alayne Adams series, each book is a standalone story, linked by the appearance of Alayne Adams.

For readers who love Catherine Ryan Hyde, Kristin Hannah or Mitch Albom.

The Truth Between Us

A make or break holiday. A love that should last a lifetime. A truth that threatens to rip them apart.

When Adaline decides to book a trip away to contemplate her failing marriage, her husband Andrew suggests he join her. As they embark on a last chance holiday to Cyprus, Adaline looks back over her life in the hope to fix what went wrong. But the past contains much pain, and a secret threatens to ruin everything. Can they confront the truth and still salvage the relationship?

The Truth Between Us is an emotional and uplifting tale about love, loss and hope.

The Initiates

A suicide note. Five lost students. One teacher who will stop at nothing to help them.

When the Principal of Knockfarraig school suggests a series of detentions for some wayward sixth year students, teacher Alayne Adams volunteers. But the discovery of a note reveals one student intends to end their life.

Taking inspiration from a book based on ancient teachings, Alayne embarks on a series of life lessons that encourages each of them to discover ways to heal their pain.**The Kybalion states, when the student is ready, the teacher will appear** but there are many obstacles in their way. Can she steer them onto a path that will change all their lives?

With characters that will have you rooting and crying for them, this contemporary, emotional novel set in Ireland, will leave you inspired.

The Initiation Of Alayne Adams

What breaks you, can also make you.

Torn between partying with her friends and doing the right thing, Alayne's life lacks any direction. Until an incident leaves her spiralling. Left with nowhere to turn, Alayne struggles to find her way. But an encounter in a library opens up new possibilities and a chance to learn. Can Alayne change or will old habits prove too hard to resist?

Printed in Great Britain
by Amazon

10270187R00079